Praise for *Defying the Odds* by Kele Moon

Reviewer's Choice Award! "I was invested and rooting for these two characters to have their happily ever after together."

— Tangie, *Two Lips Reviews*

"...absolutely worth the read and will make a wonderful addition to any erotic romance reader's collection."

— *The Long and Short of It Reviews*

"I practically devoured this book!"

— *Under the Covers Book Blog*

"...a sweet, tender, and naughty at times romance..."

— Jess, *Happily Ever After Reads*

"...I was awestruck by the amazing story..."

— *The Book Whisperer*

"*Defying the Odds* is both heartwarming and erotic, with sizzling sex and lovable characters."

— Donna, *You Gotta Read Reviews*

"Ms. Moon's writing is both candid and captivating, pulling the reader into the emotional highs and lows of the characters she creates."

— Amy, *Fiction Vixen Book Reviews*

LooseId®

ISBN 13: 978-1-61118-829-5
BATTERED HEARTS: DEFYING THE ODDS
Copyright © June 2012 by Kele Moon
Originally released in e-book format in December 2011

Cover Art by Valerie Tibbs
Cover Layout and Design by April Martinez

DISCLAIMER: Many of the acts described in our BDSM/fetish titles can be dangerous. Please do not try any new sexual practice, whether it be fire, rope, or whip play, without the guidance of an experienced practitioner. Neither Loose Id nor its authors will be responsible for any loss, harm, injury or death resulting from use of the information contained in any of its titles.

This book is an original publication of Loose Id. Each individual story herein was previously published in e-book format only by Loose Id and is a work of fiction. Any similarity to actual persons, events or existing locations is entirely coincidental.

Printed in the U.S.A. by
Lightning Source, Inc.
1246 Heil Quaker Blvd
La Vergne TN 37086
www.lightningsource.com

BATTERED HEARTS:
DEFYING THE ODDS

Kele Moon

Chapter One

"For you."

Clay looked at the small blue plate placed in front of him, his usual scowl growing deeper. "I didn't order this."

"It's a gift."

Clay's gaze snapped to the new waitress. He eyed the attractive blonde in surprise. "For what?"

She gave him a broad smile that made her green eyes glow bright and vibrant beneath her black-rimmed glasses. "For Thanksgiving," she said, her voice soft and musical to his ears. "I saw you were eating alone, and I thought, that man needs a piece of pumpkin pie."

"Oh."

He glanced back at the plate, resisting the urge to gag. He swallowed hard, choosing instead to focus on the warm feeling in his chest. He was oddly touched by the gift, simple though it might be. With the exception of his best friends, Wyatt and Jules, this waitress was the first person in a very long time that bothered to do something nice for him without expecting him to sweat or bleed in return.

She turned to leave, but he didn't want her to. He liked the pretty waitress with her sparkling eyes and thick hair wrapped up in a bun on top of her head that showed every color of blonde imaginable. He thought her glasses were charming and her figure was lush. Full hips, even fuller breasts, she looked sort of like a very huggable angel. The fluorescent lights framed her beautiful, round face with deep dimples that magically appeared when she smiled. Everything about her was soft and innocent in a way most of the women he knew would never be.

Without thinking, he reached out with lightning-fast reflexes. He grabbed her wrist before she could get too far, making her jump in shock.

Clay winced at her sharp reaction, knowing he was intimidating whether he wanted to be or not. "I'm sorry."

"'S okay," she said, her smile back, bright and happy once more. "I'm jumpy sometimes, but that's not your fault."

"I wanted to say thank you," he said, trying very hard to put emotion in his usually gruff voice. "No one's ever done this for me."

"Bought you a piece of pie?"

"No." He felt his cheeks heat, and he looked to the pie in an effort to hide. "Nobody's just nice to me, for free, without, you know, expecting something for it."

"Sweetie, you keep being sweet and I'm gonna have to buy your dinner, and between you and me, I can barely afford my own dinner, let alone feeding a big guy like you." She squeezed his hand, making him realize he was still holding on to her wrist. "So you enjoy your pie. Happy Thanksgiving."

Clay nodded his agreement and reluctantly let go. He bit his lip against doing something stupid like asking her on one of those dates real people had with flowers and candlelit dinners, or just simply blurting out he thought she looked like an honest to God angel in that waitress uniform.

Rather than gawk at the waitress, which was what he really felt like doing, he focused his attention on the pie, trying to decide if big bites would make it easier to choke down or small ones would lessen the impact.

He tried a small bite first as the chime of a bell signaled someone entering Hal's Diner, one of the few places to eat in the small town of Garnet and the only one currently open on Thanksgiving. Despite the lack of choices for the holiday, Hal's was still empty save a few bachelors.

Clay knew what lost soul had walked in without looking, and turned his focus back to the dreaded pie.

"Happy Thanksgiving, Sheriff."

"Happy Thanksgiving, Judy," came the upbeat, typically charismatic reply. "What does a hardworking sheriff have to do for a cup of coffee? Damn, but it's cold out there. Where's summer when ya need it?"

"Gonna be a nasty winter," Judy agreed, sounding equally disheartened. "Take a seat. I'll bring it to you. Are ya gonna catch a quick bite?"

"Sure, bring me whatever turkey special Hal's dishing up. You know I can't stay away from ya, darling. Having you serve me is always the highlight of my night."

"Hush." Judy laughed, sounding pleased. "You know I'm taken."

"Tell Jerry he better spoil you rotten or I'm gonna steal you right out from under him."

Clay rolled his eyes, deciding he'd rather eat pumpkin pie than listen to this shit. He was poking at it with his fork when a large, ominous shadow darkened his table. "Wyatt."

"Is that pumpkin pie?" Wyatt asked, scooting into the booth seat across from Clay and tossing his hat on the table.

"So what if it is?" Clay frowned at his best friend, who was running a hand through his blond hair, forcing away the unnatural wave caused from his hat.

Handsome and cocky as ever, Wyatt gave him a bemused smile. "But you hate pumpkin pie."

"Yeah, I know that." Clay scowled. "You think I don't know I hate it?"

Wyatt gave him a look. "Then why are you eating it?"

"That new waitress brought it," Clay explained, the reminder compelling him to take another bite. He choked, forcing himself to swallow it. "Christ."

"You've officially taken one hit too many," Wyatt said in exasperation, turning to Judy when she showed up with his cup of coffee. "Darling, dontcha have something else back there besides pumpkin pie?"

"We got praline," Judy offered, her cheeks still flushed beneath her freckles. The redhead was always pink-cheeked when Wyatt was around. "You want it before your dinner?"

"Nah, it ain't for me." Wyatt gestured to Clay. "He hates pumpkin pie. I dunno why he let her serve it to him. Get him a piece of praline."

"No, it's all right," Clay said quickly, not wanting the new waitress to know he'd sent it back. He'd rather choke down the whole thing. "I like it."

"Bullshit." Wyatt reached across the table and pulled the plate away when Clay took another stubborn bite of the pie, only to gag on it a second time. "Look at that. He can't even swallow it to prove a point."

"I'll get you a different piece, Powerhouse." Judy grabbed the plate off the table and turned away before he could complain.

"You're an asshole," Clay snapped at his best friend when Judy was out of earshot. "I was eating the damn pie. I ain't bothering you. Why the fuck do you always have to run that big mouth of yours?"

"You were gonna puke on my dinner," Wyatt said by way of explanation. "You need to tell the doc you're losing touch."

Clay huffed in response and looked across the diner to see Judy walk behind the counter. She handed the plate to Hal through the window. Clay was hoping to God they didn't tell the new waitress he hated pumpkin pie so intensely he couldn't eat it even when he attempted to swallow it down using steel will, which was something he usually had in spades.

He cringed when the pretty blonde walked behind the counter just as Hal put a fresh piece of praline pie through the window that separated the front of the diner from the kitchen. Judy said something to the new waitress, who looked at Clay and Wyatt before she turned back and grabbed the new plate instead of Judy.

"I hate you," Clay growled at Wyatt.

"Shoot." Wyatt laughed, stirring his coffee as he worked at adding several packs of sugar to it. "If I had a dollar for every time you said that, I wouldn't be spending Thanksgiving breaking up the Henleys' annual domestic disturbance. Every damn holiday, they get into it. You'd think the lot of 'em would figure out they hate each other and stop planning get-togethers. Frank had to take Derrick up to Mercy General. I think Greg broke his damn ribs."

"There's worse bones to break." Clay's eyes were on the waitress as she walked up to them. Forgetting Wyatt's whining, he smiled apologetically. "I'm sorry."

"You should've told me you hated it," she said, putting the praline pie in front of him. "I wanted you to enjoy it, not gag on it."

"I'll pay for the pie," he said, entertaining the thought of breaking *Wyatt's* ribs. "I didn't wanna put you out."

"You're not putting me out." She smiled, those dimples carving their places in her rosy cheeks. "It's not like you're asking me to shovel your driveway and take out your garbage. A new piece of pie's easy."

"Still, I appreciate it," Clay said, his cheeks hot once more. "Thank you again."

"Sure." She looked to Wyatt quickly, her smile faltering. "Glad you've got company now. Hey, Sheriff."

"Miss Dylan," Wyatt said in response. Coffee abandoned, a knowing blue gaze darted from Clay to the new waitress. "How's life treating ya?"

She smoothed out her apron, fiddling with her pad and pencil rather than look at Wyatt. "Nothing exciting to report."

Giving her one of his winning grins, Wyatt asked, "You getting settled in okay?"

"Settled in fine."

Her easy smile was gone as she turned to leave, seeming unmoved by Wyatt's natural charm, which was as unique as everything else about her. Most women were susceptible to Wyatt. Then she did something truly shocking: she reached out, squeezing Clay's large bicep through his long-sleeved cotton shirt as she walked past him to go check on recently divorced Jay Walker, sitting a few booths behind them.

"Did you just *smile* at the new waitress?"

Wyatt's voice broke through Clay's hazed thoughts, making him realize he'd actually watched her walk off and was craning his neck to see her talking and smiling at Jay. Feeling a bit like walking over there and punching poor Jay in the face, Clay decided to eat his pie and ignore Wyatt.

Problem was, Wyatt was hard to ignore. Especially when he was sitting across from him grinning like a fool and kicking his feet back against his seat, making a *thump, thump, thump* noise he knew would irritate the hell out of Clay.

He couldn't help but lift his head and bark at Wyatt, "What?"

"Nothing," Wyatt said with a laugh of disbelief. "Just seemed like you were mighty sweet and cozy with Hal's new waitress."

Clay scowled. "I ain't sweet."

"I heard you say both thank you and sorry in less than a minute. Not to mention those pearly whites you were flashing," Wyatt argued, grin still wide and shrewd. "Forget praline, I think ya wanna bite of Miss Dylan's pie."

Clay turned around, eyeing the waitress as she walked away from Jay's table, making sure she hadn't heard Wyatt. His head whipped back around to glare at the powerfully built cop. Broad shoulders, massive arms, Wyatt was one of the biggest, toughest men in Garnet, and that was saying something. The only guy who'd probably get better betting odds in a fight just happened to be sitting across from him.

"How 'bout I take a bite outta you," Clay shot back in a low and vicious voice.

"Nah, I don't swing that way." Wyatt took a long drink of his coffee, seeming undisturbed by the fury directed at him. "Thanks for asking, though."

Sometimes having a friend nearly as big and tough as him was a major annoyance. Clay was used to people bowing to his anger. "You keep grinning like that and Frank's gonna be taking *you* to Mercy General."

"If I fight back, do I get a locker room bonus?" Wyatt asked as if considering it.

"Fuck off," Clay growled, going back to his pie because intimidation wouldn't work on Wyatt.

"Clay, listen." Wyatt sighed, leaning forward to set his coffee cup on the table. His gaze became softer as he lowered his voice. "That sweet little waitress ain't for you. Stick to the groupies. They love you."

Clay cringed at the mention of groupies, biting his tongue against pointing out he had never liked those harsh, demanding women. Especially when he thought of the soft and kind Miss Dylan. He turned around, watching her talk to Judy, admiring the way the white apron hugged her hips.

"She doesn't like fighters."

Wyatt's voice cut through his fantasies, and Clay turned back to him. "What?"

"She came into the station when she first got here last week. Wanted us to know she'd filed a restraining order against her ex-husband before she left Cleveland. He used to beat on her. She moved to Garnet because she figured it was about as Bumfuck and hidden as you can get," Wyatt said in a concerned voice, casting sideway glances to the back of the diner where the waitresses were still talking. "Dumb-ass Harvey made the mistake of telling her I used to fight in the UFC. You know, so she'd see we had it handled, and she ain't said more than a few words to me since."

"Someone used to beat on her?" Clay growled. "And he's still after her?"

"I dunno the details. She seemed to feel like he was a real danger, enough to move here of all places." Wyatt took another sip of his coffee, his tall frame still hunched low over the booth as he spoke to Clay. "You get why it wouldn't work out, dontcha? Why a UFC

Hall of Fame heavyweight might not be her ideal man?"

Yeah, Clay got it, and he knew Wyatt was right. It wasn't even a shock to his system. He was too rough around the edges, too mean, too big and intimidating. Nice girls didn't fuck guys like him—groupies did.

He tried not to dwell on it. After all, he didn't even know her first name, and it wasn't like him to get sentimental. Instead he ate his pie while Wyatt quickly changed the subject. He ran his mouth about work, about Clay's odds in the upcoming fight, talking about training and the Cuthouse Cellar Training Center Clay co-owned with Wyatt and his sister, Jules. Wyatt was a real chatterbox, just rattling on like he did when he felt it was his place to fill an uncomfortable void. Clay listened, grunting when he thought it was appropriate, all the while ignoring the feeling of loss that settled in his stomach.

* * * *

"Forty-four dollars, give or take a few cents," Melody said, straightening the ones and fives she pulled out of her apron. "That ain't half bad on Thanksgiving."

"Ain't half bad at all," Judy agreed, sitting across from her counting her change. When she finished sliding the small pile of nickels into her hand, she looked up at Melody. "I round up to forty-two. Dang, you beat me."

Melody grinned. This was the first time she'd managed to beat Judy, who was a very popular waitress. Everyone in Garnet knew her, and countless regulars requested her. To beat her a week into her new job felt like a good sign when the competition was nothing but friendly.

"I forgot I gotta pay for the pie I bought Sheriff Conner's big buddy," Melody said, her shoulders slumping at the realization. "I guess you win after all."

"Nah," Judy said with a laugh. "You won fair and square. Looks like I'm mopping tonight. Silverware's all yours."

Melody wasn't going to argue. She'd worked the past five nights and lost the tip competition every single time. Her arms were aching from all the mopping because Hal's Diner was a big place—especially when you were mopping it at eleven at night after working a double shift. With a bounce in her step, she happily walked into the back, where Hal stood hunched over the sink.

Big and broad, with back muscles that clenched from his work, Hal was one of the few men who could look scary washing the dishes. He was the strong-and-silent type. No charming smile, no easy banter. He was gruff and all business.

Melody had liked him instantly.

Men like Hal, who only said their peace and nothing else, were easy for Melody to be around. They didn't put on airs trying to be something they weren't. That meant she could feel human around them instead of on edge and jumpy. She didn't trust smooth talkers like Sheriff Conner. Those snake charmers who seemed nice as could be until the doors closed and they started using their wives for punching bags.

When the sheriff had opened his mouth at the police station, Melody recoiled. He was too handsome, too cocky, too certain of his own charm and winning personality. Justin, her ex-husband, was slick as a slippery eel, but everyone thought him handsome and charming like the sheriff. Her mother used to say Justin could sell ice to Eskimos, and it was pretty darn close to the truth. If Melody never met another charming man, it wouldn't be too soon.

"I won," she announced as she stepped up next to Hal by the sink. "Silverware's mine tonight."

Hal snorted, shaking his head as a reluctant grin tugged at his lips. "I don't believe it. Judy never loses."

"No, it's true," Melody assured him as she started gathering up the silverware he'd already washed, searching for it in the hot water dyed blue with disinfectant tablets. She tossed a handful of forks into a well-worn white strainer. "By two whole dollars. Course, I still gotta pay you for those pieces of pie, but Judy didn't think they counted. That's mighty sporting of her."

"I dunno why you're buying Powerhouse dessert." Hal grunted as he went back to work on the dishes. "Boy could buy all of Garnet, pave it over, and make it his own personal parking lot. He's got more money than God, and you were living out of your truck a week ago. Where's the sense in that?"

"He seemed lonely." Melody frowned at that information, thinking there was nothing about the tall, muscular, dark-haired man that put on airs of being more than just ordinary like the rest of them. "He doesn't look rich."

Hal lifted his head, frowning at Melody, who was elbow-deep in steaming water. "Dontcha know who he is?"

Melody shook her head as she dropped a handful of forks and spoons into the white strainer and went back to fishing for silverware. "I know everyone calls him Powerhouse."

"He's a famous UFC fighter," Hal said as if it was obvious and everyone should know him. "Probably the *most* famous. He's got six heavyweight titles, and he's set to add another one to the list."

Melody turned and pulled a face at Hal. "Are ya gonna have a moment if I admit to having no idea what the UFC is? I've heard it mentioned 'bout a hundred times this past week."

Hal let out a low whistle. "Wow, I thought everyone knew, but I guess the rest of the world's not as invested as we are. UFC is the Ultimate Fighting Championship. It's a big deal. We have an MMA training center here in town that's always hopping. It's 'bout all we got to do in this town."

Melody arched an eyebrow. "MMA?"

"Mixed Martial Arts. It's a form of fighting, like boxing only more intense. It's martial arts with wrestling and kickboxing mixed into it. Takes a real athlete to compete in the MMA circuit. Only the best of the best make it to the UFC. They're the top MMA promoter in the world."

Melody shrugged, deciding she'd have to take his word for it. "Who knew someone could make that much money doing that."

"Powerhouse's fights are always broadcast nationally. He's a big moneymaker. Has fancy sponsors and everything. You might as well get used to it. We play all the fights here, whether one of our boys is up or not."

"How many guys from Garnet are in the UFC?"

"Only Powerhouse and Slayer right now, but Slayer's still green. Wyatt used to be a fighter, but he quit before he could get far. His daddy dropped dead of a heart attack and left a sheriff job opening."

"Huh," Melody said, absorbing that information. Maybe she'd misjudged the sheriff, but she still thought him too smooth to trust. "I guess that sucks. Having to quit and watch his buddy get all the glory."

"Wyatt doesn't seem to mind too much," Hal said dismissively. "He's a sixth-generation sheriff in Garnet. It's what his people do. They're bred big and mean on purpose. We wouldn't know what to do with ourselves without a Conner in charge and keeping us in line. We're a wild bunch."

"I guess." Melody laughed, surprised at Hal, who usually didn't say much. Get him started on this fighting thing and he got real talkative, which was nice. "You'd have to be a bit wild with that many prizefighters coming out of this little town."

"Some small towns grow football players or gymnasts or swimmers. You always hear about Olympians coming from some pissant town because there ain't nothing else to do but learn a sport. So that's what Garnet produces: corn-fed, all-American, extreme fighters."

"Or marines," Melody couldn't help but observe, eyeing Hal with his buzzed blond hair, knowing he'd been a marine for several years before he got out and opened the diner. "I noticed there's lots of marine talk round here."

"That ain't a lie. Course too many of our boys been coming home in boxes lately. I'm starting to wish they'd ended up in the UFC instead. Garnet boys are a little too brass for their own good."

"Yeah," Melody agreed. "But you look like a good bunch to me. I liked that Powerhouse guy. He seemed like good stock."

"What the hell kinda sense do you have?" Hal laughed. "That boy's meaner than spit."

Melody refused to believe it. Sure he was intimidating at first glance. His eyes were dark as sin, and he was one of the biggest men she'd ever seen in person. She put him at six-five easily, with massive arms and a chest that was all muscle. He'd look out of place if there weren't a lot of big guys walking around Garnet. She wasn't real sure what they put in the water, but it seemed to make the men around here a little more built than normal. But big guys didn't bother her. Her daddy had been a big guy with a gruff disposition, and he'd secretly been one of the nicest men she'd ever known.

"I think he's just misunderstood," Melody announced, remembering the fighter's handsome smile over something as simple as a piece of pie. "Maybe he just acts mean 'cause people expect it of him."

"Sounds like you're looking for a new man to me. Ain't you had enough of 'em? Showing up here homeless and looking for a job 'cause of a nasty ex-husband should do you in on all of us."

"That's the truth," Melody agreed readily. "But just 'cause I picked a nasty one doesn't mean I can't make friends. I'm trying real hard not to hold his mistakes against the whole lot of ya. I'm not gonna be scared 'cause of him. There are good men in the world. You're a good man. You gave me a job faster than I could say, 'I'm broke.' Then you got your buddy Terry to rent me that cottage with nothing but an IOU to give him. You're sweet as can be."

Hal laughed. "If ya say so."

"I do." Melody tucked the strainer under her arm and walked past Hal, squeezing his big bicep more as a reassurance to herself than him. She needed to know she could still touch men, that muscles and brawn didn't intimidate her. It was her statement to the world that she wasn't scared, and she felt good about it. "I'm gonna get this silverware rolled, 'cause I'm dead on my feet."

"Been working too hard. You don't need to work all those double shifts."

"That's the only way I'm gonna catch up," Melody reminded him, keeping to herself that working hard meant she slept deeper, which freed her from the nightmares that still haunted her.

She grabbed a stack of napkins and headed out to the dining room. Christmas music lilted over the speaker system. She enjoyed it as she worked on polishing the silverware, then rolling up a knife, fork, and spoon into each of the large napkins, getting them ready for breakfast the next morning.

She'd worked as a waitress off and on for years, and she liked this prep job more than others. There was comfort in the monotony of rolling silverware, and Melody fell into a strange trance as she worked. There were no unhappy thoughts, certainly none of the fear that had been her companion for so long. She felt free and at peace because of it. Judy's humming along to Bing Crosby's "Twelve Days of Christmas" as she worked at mopping the front of the restaurant filtered past Melody's work mind-set, and it solidified her feeling of well-being.

For the first time in a long time, Melody felt like she finally belonged somewhere.

Chapter Two

Clay would have cursed if he had a chance to catch his breath. As it was, he growled from the pain radiating from his groin after a vicious knee to the balls courtesy of Sheriff Wyatt Conner.

Wyatt ignored Clay's fury, following with a body shot to the liver. Clay actually found himself wavering. He was as shocked as anyone when he fell to his knees. Then he was feeling the full force of Wyatt's striking ability, seeing stars from the powerful, lightning-fast hits that had always been his trademark. When Wyatt got him flat on the mat and nailed him with an elbow, Clay nearly tapped out to prevent an injury that might be difficult to recover from.

"Damn it, Wyatt! Lay off!" Shouts echoed outside the cage from Clay's coaches. "You're just his training partner. You're not supposed to crack his skull before a fight!"

The hell with it. Clay wasn't giving Wyatt the satisfaction. His skull was thick enough to recover. Rather than tap, Clay wrestled for the dominant position. Being on the mat wasn't an issue. He had a balanced skill set, but Clay was a ground-and-pound fighter all the way. The mat was his home, and if he ever got tired of the UFC, he could teach jujitsu for the rest of his days. He had a sixth-degree black belt to prove it.

Wyatt was a different fighter. His bedroom walls were lined with karate belts rather than jujitsu belts and wrestling trophies. He liked all forms of boxing, but grappling had always been his weak point, and Clay used that to his advantage. Wyatt was the one who'd taught Clay long ago that even the strongest sprawl-and-brawl fighter could fall to an experienced wrestler. Pinned on the mat, with Clay's forearm choking the air out of them, there wasn't much they could do with their fancy kickboxing skills.

Ignoring the pain, he wrestled to gain the upper hand while Wyatt tried to jab at him, but it was already pointless. Clay decided he was winning. They were on the mat. He gained the dominant position quickly. Feeling vindictive, he wanted to win on Wyatt's stomping ground just to throw it in his face later. He fought to get back to his feet while keeping a good hold of Wyatt, whose massive body felt like nothing under the weight of his anger. When he finally stood, he pushed Wyatt against the cage. Then he started punching hard enough to feel his knuckles through his glove from the force of the impact. His fist flew sharp and fast, really pounding Wyatt, letting a long night of frustration flow out through his fists.

"Hey, hey, hey! Don't kill the sheriff! We need him!"

Fuck that; if he was going to spend this morning getting stitches, Wyatt was too. When Wyatt slid down the cage to his knees on the mat, Clay was on him, wrestling once more. He got Wyatt into a naked choke hold, locking his right arm around his neck and sliding his left arm across his nape. Clay pushed his head against Wyatt's, cutting off his ability to escape when he couldn't reach around and pull Clay's arms off him.

"Tap, you low-hitting motherfucker!" Clay mumbled through his mouth guard as he tightened his hold, cutting off Wyatt's air supply.

Wyatt tapped.

Clay let him go and fell onto his back, his chest rising and falling from the exertion. He could feel his heartbeat throbbing at his temples, setting off pain sensors in every sensitive place his best friend had hit. His side hurt; his balls hurt; his head was pulsating in pain.

"That was amazing." Wyatt panted next to him, his bloody, spit-filled mouth guard in his gloved hand because he could never wait more than two seconds to pull the thing out. "A fucking thing of beauty."

Clay grunted his agreement. He loved this sport. He loved the Cuthouse Cellar Training Center that had grown into a dream facility for Mixed Martial Arts fighters. Most of all, he loved Wyatt, who was the best training partner in the whole goddamn world.

"Man, Wellings doesn't stand a chance," Wyatt said, wheezing, struggling to get his breath back but still yammering because that's what he was best at. "I tried fighting dirty like him, and you still got me. I'm betting big money on this fight 'cause ain't nothing stopping you, Clay. Ya got it, buddy. The title's yours."

Yeah, Clay knew he had it. If he could get Wyatt when he was fighting dirty, he could certainly take down Romeo "The Gladiator" Wellings. The media played it up like Clay was finally going to fall from glory with this fight. Wellings was a little too mean, a little too hungry. It currently had everyone believing Clay was on his way out, because he wasn't as flashy. He didn't run his mouth to the cameras and ham it up for the fans. The betting odds were against him, but he didn't really give a shit. He knew what he was capable of.

"Damn, it's a good thing we're keeping the cameras out of the Cellar," Tony Hartings, one of Clay's coaches, announced as he walked into the eight-sided cage they'd installed in the Cuthouse Cellar to match the conditions of a real fight. "'Cause that was three rounds of nasty to watch. Wellings's camp might change their tune if they saw that."

"Don't count on it. Wellings is one cocky New York bastard. I can't wait to watch Clay lay into him." Wyatt rolled onto his side with a groan and reached up to wipe at the corner of his eye. His fingers came away bloody, and he lifted his head to Tony. "Christ, I gotta work in a few hours."

"You need some stitches," Tony said with a wince. "I dunno why you two insist on this level of training. I think you're both certifiable. You kick the bloody shit out of each other for the fun of it."

Wyatt grinned despite his split lip, showing off bloodstained teeth. "You say that like it's a bad thing. In this sport, ya gotta have a little crazy."

"They been like this since they were kids," Jasper Curtis said, coming into the ring behind Tony. "They've been beating each other bloody, black, and blue since middle school. It's amazing both of them don't have permanent brain damage."

Clay pulled out his mouth guard, holding it in his fingerless glove. He blinked up at the lights on the ceiling, finding them haloed and hazed in a way that was familiar. "I think I got a concussion."

"I'm awesome," Wyatt announced, sounding pleased to hear it. He fell onto his back once more, bleeding onto the mat and contemplating the ceiling for one long moment. "Think I got one too. I'm seeing angels round those lights."

Clay smirked. "I guess that means I'm awesome."

"Sure enough," Wyatt agreed. "No driving today. Looks like Harvey's off desk duty. I'll have my own personal chauffeur courtesy of the fine taxpayers of Garnet. I love being the boss."

"I know you do." Clay grunted because talking was hurting him. He might have a few bruised ribs. "But Jules is gonna tear into you for putting her on the phones."

Jules might be Wyatt's sister, but she was also the only lawyer for two towns. She didn't have time to scratch her ass, let alone cover the phones at the station. Every time Wyatt was forced to turn to her as backup, she got pissed off to the point of violence.

"Eh, she's all right," Wyatt said dismissively. "That girl better do what I tell her to. I'm the head Conner in charge.

Despite his ribs, Clay laughed. Wyatt really must have water on the brain to say that with a whole handful of witnesses to hear him. Someone, probably

Clay, was going to tell Jules, and that would make stitches and a concussion the least of Wyatt's problems.

* * * *

Melody realized she might need a day off after all.

Facing her sixth double, she turned off her truck in the employee parking lot and blinked tired eyes at the back of Hal's Diner. Her breath puffed out, clearly visible in the cold morning air since the heater in the truck had decided to give out. Right now it was uncomfortable; in another month it was going to be a huge issue.

She grew up in a small town about six hours outside Garnet. Melody knew how cold their winters were, and wasn't looking forward to dealing with the lack of heating. She needed to get the truck fixed. She needed a lot of things and couldn't afford to let a little exhaustion get the best of her.

Melody stuffed her frozen hands deep into the pockets of her jacket, which was old but blissfully warm. It made her think of coffee and how desperately she needed a cup of it. The cottage she'd lucked into came partially furnished, but it didn't have a coffeemaker.

She got out of the truck, thinking of Hal's coffee, which was coffeehouse delicious instead of diner crappy like every other restaurant she'd worked for. Everything Hal made was astonishingly good. He was one of those special people who had the gift of making the ordinary extraordinary. Melody considered herself incredibly fortunate to work for him, and she'd managed to cheer herself up with that thought as she pulled open the back door, letting in an icy draft.

"Whew, shut it quick!" Mary, a pretty, dark-haired waitress who worked the morning shift, shuddered as she worked at gathering up glass containers of maple syrup. "Christ on a stick, it's cold. Every year Mr. Frost seems to jump up and bite us in the ass when we least expect it. Morning, darling."

"Morning." Melody pushed the door fully shut, kicking at the corner that sometimes stuck. "I need some coffee. If I don't get some java in me, y'all will be peeling me off the floor."

"Then by all means." Mary gestured with two bottles of syrup in her hands to the front of the diner where the coffeepots were. "Go get yourself some. You worked the night shift. Just focus on getting woke up. I got this."

Melody stuffed her hands back into her coat, still fighting to warm up after the cold ride to work. Ignoring the bell chiming the arrival of customers, she headed to the coffeemakers lined up behind the counter.

"Morning," Hal called through the window from his place in front of the flattop as he prepped for the morning rush. "You gonna work in that jacket?"

"I'll take it off in a minute." Melody reluctantly pulled her hands out of her pockets to pour herself a cup of much-needed coffee. "I'm 'bout frozen. The heat's broke in the truck."

"Gotta get that fixed," Hal said in concern. "I'd offer to look at it, but I'm a terrible mechanic."

"Yeah, but you can make a meat loaf to die for." Melody grinned. "I usually hate it. That's a God's honest gift you've got."

"Ain't that the truth? Hal could make cat food taste good," Mary offered, walking out of the back with a tray of maple syrups to put on the tables. Her sneakers skidded on the linoleum as she pulled up short and gasped. "Good Lord! What'd y'all do to our sheriff?"

Melody turned, raising her eyebrows as she spied Sheriff Conner standing at the counter, waiting to be seated. He wore large, gold-rimmed sunglasses that were stereotypically police officer, but they still didn't hide the line of stitches above his eyebrow. Bruises decorated his jawline, and his lip was swollen, with another row of black stitches running down the center of it.

His face was painful to see. Melody couldn't help but wince, feeling terrified to look at his buddy standing next to him. Clay Powers's broad back was to the counter. His head dipped down, a black baseball hat pulled low over his eyes, hiding his face from view. Against her will, Melody found herself admiring the massive line of his shoulders underneath his jacket. He was one fine specimen of man, his short hair near black, his jaw strong, his nose surprisingly straight considering what he did for a living. At least it had been straight the last time she saw him. She'd be genuinely heartbroken if he'd damaged that nice male nose permanently.

"Ain't they pretty?" came a dour female reply behind the sheriff.

"Sure enough." Mary shook her head, still balancing the tray on her shoulder as she walked around the counter. "But you're looking mighty nice today, Jules. I like that suit."

"Thanks. I thought I was going to the office till my dumb-ass brother got his skull beat in—again. Now I'm stuck working at the station all day. I told 'em the least they could do was buy me breakfast."

"Lemme just get these out, and then I'll get y'all some coffee," Mary said as she started placing the syrups on each one of the tables. "You're about five minutes too early."

"I want the new girl's section."

Melody stopped drinking her coffee at the low mumble next to the sheriff, whose buddy still stood there with his back to Melody as if he'd forgotten she existed. But Clay obviously hadn't, and she took another sip of coffee to hide her smile. She wasn't just pleased to finally have a customer request her, but this customer in particular caused a fluttering in her stomach that worked at warming her up far more efficiently than the coffee. No matter how she had chastised herself, she thought of the handsome fighter all night after work. She even met up with him in her dreams, when usually it was her ex-husband and nightmares that greeted her when she closed her eyes.

For the first time in a very long time, Melody found herself genuinely attracted to a man, and she savored the feeling. It didn't even matter if he returned her feelings or not. She was just grateful she could still have them. She'd worried for years that she'd never look at a man again and feel that pulse of sexual excitement currently thrumming through her bloodstream as if it'd never left to begin with.

The sheriff's eyebrows shot up over his sunglasses as he turned to his friend. "Clay—"

"I'm buying, ain't I?" Clay interrupted before the sheriff could argue. "Unless you'd like to foot the bill."

"Hey, Mary, darling," the sheriff called out. "You mind if we sit in the other section seeing as how Miss Dylan's in need of work on her truck? I guess Clay figures she needs the cash."

"Don't mind at all," Mary said easily. "She's got the window booths."

The sheriff suddenly gasped and rubbed his ribs after a lightning-fast elbow jab from Clay. "Christ, what was that for? You know my ribs are bruised to hell and back."

"You're lucky they ain't broken." Clay growled and then jabbed him another time for good measure before he turned and walked over to Melody's section of tables.

Melody winced for the sheriff when he leaned over, grabbing his ribs once more, revealing a beautiful blonde woman behind him. Her shoulder-length hair was thick and wavy. Unlike Melody's sandy blonde, this woman had genuinely golden hair that didn't seem to be bleached. In her knee-length, fur-lined peacoat and red pantsuit, she was one of the most pressed, put-together females Melody had seen in Garnet. She looked like she'd walked off the pages of a magazine, certainly more city than country. But her fancy clothing didn't stop her from reaching up and smacking the sheriff's head.

"Your mouth," the pretty woman snapped before turning to follow after Clay. "It's always running twenty feet ahead of that dented brain of yours."

The sheriff gripped the counter, taking a deep breath before he lifted his head to look at Melody. "I guess I wasn't supposed to let on we heard you talking about the heat in your truck being broke."

Melody shrugged. "It *is* broke. Lying about it and putting on airs ain't fixing it any faster."

"I sorta wish you'd said that 'bout a minute sooner." He grunted, still wheezing through the pain. "I'm gonna go sit down now."

"I'll get out of my jacket and bring the coffee."

"Sounds good." The sheriff did a thumbs-up, still looking miserable when he turned and started walking to the booth his sister and Clay sat at.

Melody laughed, having to reluctantly admit the sheriff was hard to hate. Something about him was endearing, even if she found his devilish charm more than a little off-putting. He wasn't her type of man, not anymore, not ever if she was being honest, but he seemed nice enough.

She took a couple more big gulps of coffee, ignoring the burn to her mouth as she walked to the back. She shrugged out of her jacket, then hung it up in the corner next to the other employees' hats and coats before she found a pad underneath the server station. Deciding she'd work on gathering her other supplies after she'd gotten their order, she dashed to the front of the diner with more enthusiasm than she should. She was probably being pathetic and obvious, but who the hell cared? That fighter had her feeling young and alive when she'd felt worn-out and beaten for so long.

"Slow down; they ain't going anywhere. We're not even officially open," Mary scolded when Melody quickly collected three cups in one hand and a steaming pot of coffee in the other. "No sense getting flushed and flustered over those three. Not a one of 'em can cook. They're Hal's customers for life."

Not bothering to explain her excitement, Melody rushed up to the booth. The sheriff sat next to his sister, his hat on the table next to him as he smoothed out his hair. But Melody didn't bother to pay more attention than that. She put the coffee cups down, asking, "Coffee?"

"Yes, please," the sheriff said quickly. "We've been up since four."

"That's painful to hear." Melody filled up the sheriff's cup and his sister's, who nodded to Melody's silent offering, before she turned to Clay. She studied his face beneath the low brim of his hat, knowing she was probably gawking like a lovesick fool. He had a small line of stitches at the corner of his right eye and his face was showing bruises and swelling, but the damage wasn't terrible. "You don't look that bad. I was worried you'd look as rough as the sheriff."

"Well." Clay swallowed hard, a smirk trying to tug at his lips. He pulled off his baseball hat, running his fingers through inky hair. He turned back to her, giving her a real smile despite his swollen bottom lip. "That's 'cause I won."

"Glad to hear it." Melody beamed as she filled his cup, her cheeks hurting from the happiness she knew just spilled out of her, making her totally obvious to everyone. It was a good thing he was well-known and probably used to girls crawling all over him, because she was certainly starry-eyed. "Hal said you're real good, like famous and all. That's exciting."

"Is it?" he asked, his smile becoming bemused as he frowned at her.

"Well, yeah." She studied his bruised face, trying to memorize his features. Clay was starkly masculine but not traditionally handsome like the sheriff, more rough around the edges in a way that appealed to her. His eyes were so dark it was hard to see his pupils, and he had a day's beard growth that made him look even more rugged and attractive. "I mean, I don't know much 'bout fighting or anything 'cept bruises like those hurt, but I'm glad you're good at it."

A scowl carved a familiar pattern into his forehead as if accustomed to being there. "Why would you be glad if you don't know nothing 'bout it?"

"'Cause I'm happy for you," Melody said, still awed and bubbling with exhilaration over how inexplicably drawn she was to this man. She felt normal and womanly and blissfully free from her demons. She should probably go back to work before she embarrassed herself, but she felt like a slab of metal being pulled closer to this big, surly fighter like he was a magnet made just for her. "You're the best at something. There ain't a bigger accomplishment than that, is there?"

"I dunno." He looked to his coffee, frowning at it for one long moment. "I guess that *is* something."

"A whole lot of something," she agreed, forcing her brain to start working again. She set the coffeepot down on the table. "Anyway, I better take your order before I stand here bugging you all day."

"You don't bug me," he said quickly. "I like listening to you talk. Your voice is pretty. Sounds nice, like music or something."

"Really?" She beamed, a blush burning her cheeks from the compliment. She pulled her pad out of her apron and fished for a pencil as she fought the flustered feeling tightening her chest from the compliment. "Well, you're the first one to ever say so. My ex-husband used to say my yapping was like nails on a chalkboard. Course, he was mostly city and my accent bothered him. I guess it don't bother you."

"No." Clay grunted, the scowl back. "Don't bother me at all."

"Anyway." Melody took a deep breath, her cheeks still burning, her brain scrambled from the simple compliment because she didn't know how to handle kindness from a man she liked as much as Clay. Perhaps she wasn't as normal as she'd hoped, and her shoulders slumped with the realization. She turned to the sheriff and his sister to hide the disappointment in herself. "What can I getcha?"

She took their order, her heart still beating the hell out of her ribs. Her breathing became rapid without warning because she'd mentioned her ex-husband and just thinking about him was enough to make her anxious. It would be a minor miracle if she got their order right, especially Clay's, who was frowning at Melody, his dark eyes studying her as he ordered his breakfast.

"Okay," she rasped once she'd gotten their order, still willing her breathing to be steady and normal as she turned to leave. She nearly jumped out of her skin when Clay grabbed her wrist, forcing her to drop her pad to the ground. She winced and, out of instinct, blurted out, "I'm sorry!"

"What'd you got to be sorry 'bout?" Clay asked her softly, letting go of her wrist when she bent to pick up the pad. "Did I say something wrong?"

"No, it's not you," she said quickly. Wanting to reassure him, she reached out to squeeze his bicep through his long-sleeved black shirt that clung to his massive arms. She could still touch him, and it felt good, better than she thought it would. It helped to clear her head. She took a cleansing breath as she admitted, "It's me. I'm just a little bit broken."

"What?" he asked, his voice low and concerned.

"Not a lot, just a little. I'm okay." She squeezed his arm again, more to reassure herself than him. Then she turned to leave but pulled up short, wanting to smack her forehead. "I'm stupid. The coffeepot. I got it. We'll get your order right quick."

"We're not worried 'bout it," Clay said as she picked up the coffeepot. "Just bring it when it's done. No sense rushing. We know we're early."

"You're sweet." She sighed, thanking God for handsome fighters named Clay. Even a glimpse of normalcy was better than none at all, and she was so incredibly grateful for it. She couldn't help but turn and give Clay a long, lingering look, thinking it was probably a good thing he was famous and out of her reach. "Thank you."

Then she left before he could say something. The coffeepot clutched tightly in her hand, she practically ran into the kitchen, deciding to give the order to Hal personally and use the moment to hide and pull herself together.

CLAY WATCHED THE pretty waitress leave. Her cheeks flushed pink, her chest heaving underneath her simple blue and white uniform as she disappeared into the back. He tried to sort out the plethora of emotions overwhelming him. Most were feelings he was unaccustomed to, like a wild need to run after her and comfort her until that panicked look left her bright green eyes, now reflecting fear underneath her glasses. Clay was the last person in the world who should be comforting anyone. Instead he searched for stable ground, thumbing through the rush of emotion until he found one he knew how to handle.

"If that ex-husband of hers shows up in Garnet, I'm gonna have him installed in the Cellar as my own personal punching bag." He felt a pulsing fury surge through his bloodstream. "Fucker."

He looked back to the front the restaurant, hoping to catch a glimpse of her, still battling with the urge to soothe away her fears. He was floundering, and he knew it. A headache and his own set of bruised ribs had him twitchy. He raised his hips, searching in the pocket of his jeans for the pain relievers the doctor had stuffed in his hand before Jules drove them to breakfast.

"Hey, Jules, you got my ibuprofen?" he asked, coming up with nothing but his wallet. He lifted his head to look at her, finding Jules stunned speechless, her jaw actually hanging open. He glanced to Wyatt, sitting next to her, who had a similar look of shock on his handsome face. "You two running a fly-catching contest or something? What're you gawking at?"

Jules's jaw clicked shut first. Ever poised, she ran fingers through her shiny hair, before she turned back to Clay. "You're sweet on her."

"So what if I am?" he barked back, feeling his cheeks heat.

"That's the worst pairing in the world, you and that jumpy little waitress. What a nightmare," Wyatt said with a sad shake of his head. "I don't think it'll work, Clay. You heard her admit it herself: she's broken."

"And I ain't?" Clay countered.

Jules's blue eyes became soft and concerned in sisterly fashion. "You're not broken, sweetie."

"Well," Wyatt argued, tilting his head as he gave his sister a look, "I wouldn't exactly put him on the normal scale of human behavior."

"You ain't on the normal scale." Jules growled, turning around to punch Wyatt's shoulder with sharp speed and painful accuracy, because Wyatt and Clay weren't the only ones with a running collection of black belts. "So you just sit there, shut up, and drink your coffee, because if you say something dumb to that sweet waitress, Clay won't have to break your ribs. I'll do it for him!"

"Fine," Wyatt said, holding up his hands in surrender. "I'll shut my trap."

"That'll be a first." Jules rolled her eyes and turned back to Clay. She gave him an encouraging smile. "She's sweet on you too, you know?"

Clay shrugged, now more than uncomfortable. He took a sip of his coffee, deciding to ignore their concern. He loved both of them. They were the only real family he had, but there were days, like today, when he wished he'd stayed in foster homes instead of setting up camp in the bedroom across from Wyatt's. Conners were a nosy, meddling lot. It was the law enforcement mentality bred into them. They had the inexplicable urge to know what was going on with everyone and everything they cared about. If their nosing unearthed something they felt needed their attention, they worked with grim determination to make it right, and both of them couldn't care less if their help was welcome or not.

"Well, I for one think it's 'bout time Clay got himself a woman," Jules announced, making her opinion known as usual. "Him liking this girl is a good thing. Means he's finally warmed up to dating."

"He dates," Wyatt said defensively.

Jules turned, giving her brother a stern look. "Last I checked, I had several degrees on my office wall. How dumb do I look?"

"He sorta dates," Wyatt amended, because no one could call Jules dumb.

"You and me both know he ain't dating those girls," Jules said sharply. "And not a one of 'em care anything 'bout him. All they're interested in is his fine body and his collection of championship belts. They're just using him. I don't like those groupies, Clay."

"No kidding," he said against the rim of his coffee. "I think I heard mention of that one time...or a million."

"So you ask the jumpy little waitress on a date, and if it don't work out"—Jules held up her hands—"at least you broke the ice. You can finally start dating real women."

"So those girls he spends time with ain't real women?" Wyatt quirked an eyebrow over the rim of his sunglasses. "What are they, then? 'Cause they look mighty womanly to me."

"I meant women with souls," Jules said sweetly before she narrowed light eyes at her brother. "You're a pig, by the way."

Wyatt turned to her, his mirrored glasses reflecting Jules's image back at her as he grinned. "Oink."

Jules pulled a disgusted face, turning back to Clay. "You're thirty-three years old. Ya can't keep pushing every decent woman away 'cause your mama left like that."

"So he should date the only person in Garnet with more issues than him?" Wyatt interjected as if considering it. "A man with crippling abandonment issues who makes a living with his fists, and a woman on the run from her abusive ex-husband who obviously used her as a punching bag. That's a *perfect* pairing."

"I gotta take a leak." Clay stood up rather than listen to their bickering. He was halfway to the bathroom before something occurred to him. He turned back around, finding Jules and Wyatt still arguing. Before he could catch a word of their debate, he leaned down, looked Jules dead in the eye, and admitted, "I ain't been with one of those groupies in over a year and a half."

"Really?" Jules asked, her eyebrows shooting up in surprise.

"Yes, really," he said with grim finality. "Now will you shut up 'bout it?"

"Yeah, I'll shut up," Jules said, positively beaming. "I wouldn't say anything to her 'bout it...even if ya had been with 'em."

"I haven't."

"Okay," Jules said, holding up her hands passively. "Glad to hear it."

Clay hoped that was enough to keep both Jules and Wyatt's mouths shut while he was gone. He wasn't more than a few feet away from the table before Wyatt said, "A year and a half? No wonder my ribs are 'bout broke, and this ain't the first time, neither."

Jules snorted. "You say it like it's my fault."

"You're always harping 'bout the groupies. The man needs some sorta stress release besides kicking the shit outta me."

Clay rolled his eyes, deciding there was nothing to be done. Let them argue. That battle was lost a long time ago. If big Fred Conner couldn't put a stop to it before he passed on, Clay sure wasn't going to fix it. He just wished they'd find another topic to argue about.

Chapter Three

"It's official. You've got an admirer."

Melody blushed, turning around to look and see if anyone was listening before she shrugged. "Nah. He's just sweet."

"Sweet on you," Judy said teasingly as she leaned against the counter, giving Melody a knowing look. "Every single shift you work, he's here. If you ain't here, he ain't here. That boy knows your schedule."

"I think she might be right," Hal offered, putting her order in the window. "I'd have never believed it, but something 'bout you got Powerhouse's attention."

"And he's a good tipper," Judy said sullenly. "If I'd known he had a soft spot for waitresses, I'd have bought him pie years ago."

"I told him to stop with all that." Melody felt her cheeks heat. "Ain't fair. He's not allowed to tip more than twenty percent."

"You need the money," Hal barked at her. "Take it if he's offering."

Melody ignored them, not wanting his food to get cold. She grabbed Clay's plate and walked around the counter. At a quarter to ten, the diner was near empty. He was her last table of the evening. She loved it when he came late, because she could spend actual time with him.

She placed Clay's plate in front of him and then helped herself to the booth seat across from him. Hidden like he was in the corner, she could sit with him free from prying eyes. That was the thing with Garnet; everyone was in everyone else's business.

"I think this town needs a movie theater." Melody pulled her legs up and rested her chin on her knees as she watched Clay eat his country-fried steak. "All they got to worry 'bout is what we're doing."

Clay lifted his gaze to hers and then leaned out of the booth, looking to the counter. When he turned back to his dinner, a smile tugged at his lips.

"They're watching us?" Melody asked, knowing the answer for herself.

"Yup." Clay grunted as he cut his meat. "Didja eat?"

"Been snacking. I'm good." Melody's eyes felt heavy, and she was half tempted to fall asleep right there at the booth. "Tell me 'bout your day."

"It's not very exciting."

"I like to hear your voice," Melody admitted, blinking tiredly at Clay. He was wearing his usual black cap pulled low over his eyes. His bruises had healed, and he was looking very handsome and rugged this evening with a day's worth of dark beard growth decorating his jaw. She couldn't help but smile as she admired him. "I think 'bout it at night, your voice, before I go to sleep. Scares away the nightmares."

He tilted his head, looking at her from under the brim of his cap. His dark eyes were soulful, penetrating as he studied her curled up in the booth across from him. Instead of saying something to make her feel dumb or weak, he just smiled and started talking.

Clay told her about his day, which was pretty uneventful. It turned out famous Mixed Martial Arts fighters spent 90 percent of their time doing Mixed Martial Arts...and eating.

If Melody ate half as much as Clay, she'd weigh seven hundred pounds, but there wasn't an ounce of fat on him. He was all muscle, and she allowed herself the luxury of admiring him. She studied the broad expanse of his chest and the flex of his powerful arm muscles beneath his shirt as his low voice washed over her, soothing her with the lull of his accent. She certainly chose right to hide out in a small town close to where she grew up. Hearing the sounds of her youth in everyone's voice was nice. If she never saw a city again, it wouldn't be too soon.

"Then Jules asked me to help out with one of the self-defense classes she teaches at the Cellar, since Wyatt was wise enough to work overtime. Said he had a domestic disturbance, but you and me know that ain't true. He was sitting at the station screwing around on the city's dime," Clay said, taking another bite of his food before he gave a half laugh. "So I spent an hour getting beat on by old ladies."

Melody smiled, letting her eyes drift closed. "Sorry I missed it."

"I think a few of those old gals was touching me inappropriately on purpose."

"Maybe I need to take me a self-defense class," Melody teased.

"I got connections at the Cellar, seeing as how I own half of it," Clay said, his voice no longer lighthearted. "You could take whatever classes ya wanted, Mel. A self-defense class ain't a bad idea."

Melody snorted. "If I find that much free time, the only thing I'm taking is a nap."

"Gimme your tips; I'll count 'em. Help ya get done early."

"Nah," she argued, her eyes still closed. She felt exhausted on a soul-deep level. "I still gotta get prep work done, and I gotta get your ticket rung up and—"

"Here, take this."

Melody blinked, finding Clay's thick, wool-lined jacket in her face. "What?"

"Take a power nap, and I'll eat slow," Clay suggested, jacket still pushed in her face as he held it across the table. He leaned out of the booth, scanning the near-empty restaurant. "Judy's still got two customers. You got a few minutes to rest."

It was a testament to how truly tired she was, because she grabbed the jacket. It smelled like Clay, warm and woodsy and masculine. She couldn't help but bury her face in the wool lining, letting his scent comfort her. It was such an overwhelming feeling she couldn't even think to be embarrassed. Life was too damn short, and something as soothing as Clay's scent surrounding her had Melody falling down on the booth bench. She buried her face in the jacket, nearly smothering herself, but it didn't matter because all the tension eased out of her.

"Don't let me get fired," she mumbled into the wool. "Wake me up if they come snooping."

"Gimme your tips. You can tell 'em you were counting."

Melody reached into her apron. She grabbed handfuls of small bills and slapped them on the counter. When she'd retrieved all the bills, she fished for the coins, setting them blindly on top of the cash to keep them in place, but she heard a few strays try to roll away as they clattered on the tabletop.

"Where's the rest of it?"

"That's it." Melody tucked her hand under her cheek and pulled her sneakered feet closer to her body so they weren't hanging out of the booth. "Pretty busy tonight. Can't be half bad, but I'll probably be mopping."

"Christ." Clay sighed over the sound of him sorting through the bills. "No wonder you're always working. This ain't nothing."

"You smell nice," Melody mumbled in response, still high on the smell of him clouding her senses and the soft feel of wool against her cheek. "Just gonna close my eyes. Wake me up before someone comes."

Clay grunted in the affirmative, and that was enough for her. She let her eyes drift closed, thinking she hadn't been this comfortable in her entire life. Melody fell into a deep, fathomless sleep almost instantly.

CLAY COUNTED MELODY'S tips while he ate. When he was done, he stared at the pile of cash that totaled eighty-eight dollars and seventy cents, realizing she'd worked since breakfast for it.

Life seemed really fucking unfair when he considered his own bank accounts, which had a truly obnoxious amount of money in them. What the hell kind of world did they live in that he made so much for fighting a few cocky bastards a year and she made so little for running around, taking care of people fifteen hours a day?

He wanted to add a few grand to that pile, but he knew from experience it wouldn't fly. That first breakfast when he'd requested Melody wait on them, he'd left her a hundred-dollar tip. He wasn't three feet into the parking lot before she was running out after him, arms bare in the cold as she thrust the big bill back at him, flat-out refusing to accept it. He'd argued and refused to take it, pointing out her truck had no heat and her jacket was near bare in spots. She'd just boldly stuffed the money into the pocket of his jeans and walked back inside, claiming it wasn't fair.

Then Clay started to get creative. He'd bribed everyone who worked at Cuthouse Cellar to eat at Hal's on her shifts and leave big tips. Three days in, Melody smelled a rat and refused to wait on *anyone* from the Cellar, including Wyatt and Jules. That's when he gave up, because more than half the town either worked for or attended classes at the Cuthouse Cellar Training Center. Swearing off the Cellar patrons and employees was the equivalent to committing waitress suicide.

Once Clay promised to lay off the tips conspiracy, Melody went back to waiting on anyone who sat in her section. Clay supposed near ninety dollars on a Wednesday was decent, but he knew she was still trying to save for her truck and furniture and rent. She owed Terry the deposit for the utilities that he'd fronted her. She owed Hal two hundred dollars he'd loaned her to get groceries and other supplies. She needed a new coat. Her sneakers had holes in the bottoms of them. She never wore gloves, and there wasn't a damn thing Clay could do about any of it because it seemed she was willing to accept at least some help from anyone but him.

"Hey, Melody, darling, Powerhouse's the last of—"

Clay leaned out of the booth, giving Judy a pleading look, and whispered, "I'll pay you a thousand dollars to let her sleep."

Clay was dead serious. He'd pay twice that to give her the few minutes of sleep she desperately needed. He was starting to worry about her driving, because she always looked two blinks away from passing out.

"No, no, I'm up." Melody shot up in the booth before Judy could respond, stray strands of blonde hair escaping her bun and framing her face. She blinked as if still trying to get her bearings. "I was just resting my eyes."

"Don't that mean sleeping?" Judy asked, giving Melody an indulgent smile. "You wanna take off? I'll do the prep work for tonight."

"No," Melody said quickly as she worked at pushing the stray wisps of hair back into place. "You ain't doing my job for me. If I'm gonna take double shifts for the extra money, then I'm gonna do all the work."

"You look like a strong wind would blow you over," Judy scolded.

"I got it." Melody scooted out of the booth, reaching over to grab Clay's jacket before she turned to him. "How much did I make?"

"Oh." Clay looked to the neat pile of money and coins he had stacked in front of him. "'Bout ninety. Eighty-eight and some change. I guess that'd make it near a hundred if you include my tip."

Melody turned to look at Judy hopefully, but her shoulders slumped when Judy winced and said, "I had the Wednesday church group tonight."

"No, it's good," Melody said, recovering easily as she handed Clay his jacket. "Thanks. The power nap worked. I feel better."

Clay grabbed her hand when she leaned over him, picking up her money and putting it in her apron. He studied Melody's angelic face, seeing dark circles under her eyes. She was still beautiful enough to haunt his dreams every night since she'd first bought him that piece of pie, but there was no question the hard work was wearing on her. He wanted to toss her over his shoulder and tie her to the bed until she stopped fighting and got some much-needed sleep.

But if there was one thing Clay understood, it was the need to fight.

"Can I help ya?" he asked softly. "I'm a good mopper, highly qualified. I mop the Cellar all the time, and those floors are pretty damn repulsive. This place ain't nothing for me."

Melody shook her head. "Ah no, Hal wouldn't—"

"Sure he would," Judy interjected. "If he's feeling inspired to work for free, Hal ain't one to complain 'bout that. After I had Stella, Jerry'd drive out here every night with the baby and do all my prep work while I sat in the back and fed her."

Clay grinned triumphantly and tossed his jacket into the booth. He pulled off his UFC baseball cap and put it on backward, letting her know he was ready to work. He squeezed Melody's hand, seeing her cheeks were flushed pink and a smile quirked at the corner of her full, pink lips.

He stood up, deliberately crowding into her personal space because being near her felt like breathing fresh air after a lifetime of choking on dust. Her head only came to his shoulder, and it left him feeling powerful and masculine in a way he found addictive. He let go of her hand only to cup her face. He gave in to the indulgence, letting his thumb sweep across Melody's cheek. He savored her smooth skin, wondering if all of her was just as silky.

His entire body tightened because he was officially obsessed with Melody Dylan, who was exotic and unique to him. All the women he spent time with were built like Jules—with strong, condensed, muscular bodies honed from years of martial arts training. The groupies were slender and fit too, thinking hard bodies were essential to gaining attention, and perhaps they were for other fighters, but not for Clay.

He liked Melody's softness and cherished the gentle curves instead of hard angles. Clay wanted to drown in her, to spend a lifetime learning her with his mouth and hands. He didn't just want to fuck her; he wanted to actually *love* her with his body in a way that had never occurred to him before Thanksgiving. It was more than her lush figure and beautiful smile. It was her soul that called out to him. Being around her felt like coming home. He could smile around her. He could laugh and feel normal in a way he never anticipated with anyone, even Wyatt and Jules, who were practically family.

When his hand slid to the back of her neck on instinct, Melody's eyes drifted closed. It'd be so easy to kiss her, to find out if that heart-shaped mouth really tasted as sweet as it looked. After days of jerking off in the shower to her image, he felt out of his mind enough to give in to the temptation.

Melody turned her cheek away before he could, not fighting his hold on her neck but opening her eyes to stare past his shoulder. Disappointment flashed brilliant green behind her black-rimmed glasses, forcing Clay to turn and look.

Judy stood there, eyes wide as she watched the two of them. Behind her, Hal was leaning out of the door to the kitchen, making his interest blatantly obvious. Clay actually moaned out loud, his cock aching with frustration as he glared at the two of them.

"This town does need a movie theater," he grumbled under his breath as he turned back to Melody.

"That ain't a lie," Melody agreed, placing a palm on his chest and pushing him away with a look of pain that told him she was hurting as badly as he was from the forced separation. "If you're dying to mop, then be my guest."

He was dying to do something else entirely, but mopping was his only outlet for the tension. Clay mopped the hell out of Hal's Diner, putting real elbow grease into getting the floors cleaned. Once the front was clean, Clay walked into the kitchen, still frustrated. He tackled the kitchen, finding those floors more appealing because of the thin coating of grease from the day's cooking. Maybe if he could get the kitchen clean, he could start thinking clearly again.

The hum of sexual energy pulsed under his skin, making him feel wild and hungry. He used to think of sex as a necessary evil, something he was forced to indulge in when his body became a little too demanding to be denied. But most days his hand was a perfectly fine companion, and he rarely if ever sought out something more than that. Now he couldn't stop thinking about it. It was making him aggravated and itchy in a way he found decidedly unappealing.

"I usually mop the kitchen." Hal interrupted Clay's internal musings. "You don't gotta do that."

"I *do* gotta do it," Clay assured him as he attacked the kitchen floor with manic vengeance.

It was either mop the floor or drag Melody into a corner and find a more carnal release for his tension, which was something he wasn't sure either of them were ready for. She had issues with men. He had issues with women. Sex could end up ruining something that had become beautiful and perfect to him.

But that simple fact didn't stop his body from throbbing for it or his mind from replaying images of how willing Melody had seemed a few minutes before. God, he was going to have to stop by the Cellar on the way home and kick the shit out of a few punching bags just to get her out of his system.

"Well, dang, boy, you do a mighty fine job, I'll give ya that," Hal said with a laugh as he finished the dishes and started working on the flattop. "I'd hire you if ya didn't already have a job."

Clay grunted, knowing anything he said would come out surly and intimidating. He had a hard time talking to people when he *wasn't* pent up with blinding sexual frustration. Now he knew it was best to just keep his mouth closed.

Someone walked into the kitchen and Hal asked, "Why are you doing the silverware?"

"'Cause I like doing 'em," Melody explained. "Judy's marrying the ketchups and filling all the shakers and sugar trays."

Clay turned, hungry just to look at her, which was sort of pathetic, but he couldn't seem to help himself. He watched Melody reaching into the blue water, pulling out handfuls of silverware and dropping it into a white strainer.

Clay leaned against the mop as he admired the way Melody looked bent over the sink, still elbow-deep in the steaming water. He couldn't help but ask, "How do you marry ketchup?"

"You perform a little condiment marriage ceremony and then fill out a buncha paperwork in triplicate," Melody said without missing a beat.

Clay laughed, his gaze running over her, hot and hungry, and he didn't give a shit if Hal was watching. "Sounds exciting."

"Oh it is," Melody assured him, dropping another fistful of silverware into the strainer. "You haven't lived till you've seen ketchups marry. Hang around long enough and you'll see a few mustards and barbecue sauces get hitched too. It's a party here every night after y'all leave."

"I gotta stay after close more often," Clay agreed.

"You keep mopping like you're doing and you're more than welcome," Melody said with a laugh. "Hal, did you see what he did with the front? I can see my reflection in those tiles."

"I don't doubt it." Hal laughed, his big arms straining from the effort of scraping the flattop in hard, fast movements. "You ever get tired of the UFC, you got a job ready and waiting for ya."

"I'd be a horrible waiter. People piss me off more often than not," Clay assured both of them. "And I sure as hell can't cook. All we got to eat back at the house are a buncha microwave meals and protein drinks."

"How come you live with Wyatt and Jules?" Melody asked.

Clay started mopping as he thought about the answer. "I guess I just never bothered to move out. The house was real lonely after Big Fred died, just weird feeling without him. I didn't have the heart to leave 'em like that even if I could afford my own place. Now I suppose I stick around to keep the two of 'em from killing each other. Habit mostly. Not so bad. They're both workaholics. Neither one of 'em are round much. I see 'em more at the Cellar than at home."

"Huh?" Hal said, sounding surprised. "I suppose that's mighty friendly of you, Powerhouse."

Clay paused in his mopping, realizing that was probably the most Hal had heard out of him—ever.

He'd just made a decision not to speak, but Melody pulled down the walls he'd been putting up for as long as he could remember just by being around him. He wasn't sure if he was happy about it or not, but it was hard to be mad at her for it. Rather than dwell on it, he focused on mopping, his arms straining from the force of his enthusiasm, because thus far he hadn't managed to work off one bit of the sexual frustration.

* * * *

"Drive carefully."

Melody nodded. Her stomach fluttered with a million emotions, and she wanted to stand there with Clay in the snow forever. She looked up at him, trying to memorize his handsome face framed in golden light from the streetlamp over the parking lot while snowflakes danced down from the heavens. Scruffy whiskers, black hair sticking out from underneath his black UFC hat still on backward, he was sinfully beautiful with his soulful eyes studying her just as closely.

She reached up and brushed at his forehead, which was still shiny with sweat. Her touch lingered and then slid down to feel the prickle of a day's worth of whiskers on his cheek. "Thank you for helping me."

"Sure." He smiled, showing off even white teeth that were almost too perfect. "Anytime."

"You have a pretty smile," she blurted out before she could stop herself, because she noticed it often. "It makes you real handsome."

"It's fake." Clay clicked his teeth together, showing them off. "Most of 'em are fake. I spend a small fortune on dental work 'cause having a buddy like Wyatt is hard on my smile. I'm always showing up in Clara's office with some sorta emergency."

Melody laughed. "Well, she does a good job. They're like movie star teeth. I need me some of those."

"I like your smile. It's beautiful. You're beautiful."

His low voice caused a zing of pleasure to dance across Melody's skin. His dark eyes ran over her once more. He was getting bolder, because his gaze lingered on her chest, exposed to the cold from her open jacket. Then he stepped into her personal space and reached for the zipper of her worn jacket, working on getting it closed for her.

"You need a new jacket."

"I know," she whispered, because she was suddenly breathless. Having him zip up her jacket felt so very intimate. Letting him do it caused a low heat to build in her stomach and spread into her arms and legs despite the cold. She closed her eyes, trying desperately to ignore the pulse of need between her legs. "I need a lot of things."

"I sorta wanna give you those things, Melody," Clay whispered, his tone husky and compelling. He slowly pulled the zipper up, letting it run over the curve of her breasts, making her feel as if she could sense the warmth of his touch through her uniform. "I wish you'd let me."

Melody took a shuddering breath, knowing they were talking about more than jackets and big tips. Why did this have to happen now? She'd never expected to find a man who affected her as Clay did. It felt like her life was a jigsaw puzzle, and Clay was the missing pieces. They just fit together so well. She felt safe and happy and whole when she was with him.

God, she wanted him.

Her body literally ached with need, and she didn't know what to do about it. Giving in to everything he was offering would be effortless if she'd allow herself the luxury of letting down her guard, but she couldn't. She hated her ex-husband for damaging her to the point that she didn't recognize hope and happiness even when it was looking her dead in the eye.

"I'm sorry," was all she could manage to whisper. Her heart hurt, and tears stung her eyes, forcing her to blink against breaking down. "I'm sorry for being me."

"Don't ever be sorry for that," Clay said with a vehemence that made Melody look up at him in surprise. He responded by reaching out to brush at the stray wisps of hair framing her face, tucking them behind her ears gently. "I think you're wonderful exactly how you are. The rest ain't that important, okay?"

A dark, cynical laugh slipped out of Melody. "Most men would say it's pretty darn important. Justin used to force me if he went more than two or three days without."

"Christ." Clay sucked in a sharp breath, his eyes wide and horrified. "Mel—"

"You coming, darling?" Judy interrupted him as she leaned against the front door of the diner. "We're done in here, and we're beat."

"Yeah," Melody called out, her cheeks hot with embarrassment and wet from tears she hadn't realized she'd lost the battle against. She wiped them hastily and reached down, squeezing Clay's big hand in hers. "Thanks for the help."

"Sure," he said, squeezing her hand back.

It showed how amazing Clay was that he didn't try to stop her and he didn't expect more of an explanation. He let her turn away and run back into the diner, and there was a huge comfort in that. He just let Melody be herself, the good and the bad, and he appeared to like every side of her. If she weren't about to break down from the pain walking away from him caused, she'd have to admit he would be very easy to fall in love with.

She dashed up the steps to the diner, forcing herself not to look back. If she did, she'd likely run back into Clay's arms, all her issues be damned.

Melody jumped past the front door Judy held open, shivering from the cold because the first week of December brought a cold front chilly enough to freeze hell. She pushed her hands tighter into her pockets, thinking she needed to bite the bullet and pay for a good pair of gloves.

"You okay?" Judy asked, frowning at Melody in concern. "You look upset."

"Oh no," Melody lied. "Just tired."

Judy gave her a dubious look but didn't say anything as she locked the front door. When they left the dining room, they met Hal, who was doing a few last-minute cleanups in the kitchen. He seemed surprised to see Melody walking out back with them.

"You're not gonna spend time with Powerhouse?" he asked.

Melody shook her head. She couldn't speak even if she wanted to, because she was fighting tears again. She looked to her feet, seeing the black skid marks on her white sneakers, and knew she needed to take a cup of bleach to them.

"Come on," Hal said, putting a big arm over her shoulder, ushering her out the back door. "What you need is a morning off."

"Oh no," Melody argued as the cold slapped her in the face once more. "I need the money."

"You need a morning off," Hal reiterated. "I'll call Fran to fill in for the early shift. Sleep in. It'll make all the difference in the world."

Feeling a little too heartsick to argue, Melody just nodded as she walked with Hal, letting his big body offer her warmth. Maybe she did need a morning to herself, and sleeping in was too tempting to pass up. She'd get some extra rest and come in for the night shift feeling like a new woman.

"Okay." Melody gave Hal a genuine smile when they stopped in front of her old truck. "So I'll sleep in 'cause the boss told me to."

"That's right." He squeezed her shoulder once more. "Now get in that truck and get home before you catch your death."

Melody couldn't argue with that, not when the cold was stinging her face and burning her ears. She needed to buy a hat to go with the gloves, and she focused on that thought rather than the heartache over Clay welling up in her chest.

Problem was, her hands were so frozen she dropped her keys into the snow as she tried opening the truck. She officially needed a morning to herself; there was no denying it as she bent down and fished for her keys in the snow. Her hands burned. It would be a miracle if she didn't sit there and start crying.

"Whatcha doing?" Hal asked as he opened his car door.

"Dropped my keys." Melody was still feeling for her keys, squinting past the tears and cold and darkness to find them. When her fingers closed around icy metal, she called out, "Found 'em!"

"Get home," Hal called back, obviously determined to get home, get warm, and then get to sleep because he worked more than Melody did.

"Night, darling," Judy said and then shut her car door.

Melody waved as Judy started her car. Her numb fingers searched for the right key as Hal's car also started up. She found it and finally opened the truck door, knowing Hal was waiting for her to get into the truck before he left. She waved to him in assurance as she crawled into the truck and pulled the door closed. She locked it out of habit and then leaned over to the glove compartment. She used to have gloves in there last winter. There was always the vain hope they were hiding. After searching through the contents, she sighed, her breath a puffy white mist inside the cab. She was going to have to pay for new gloves.

There was no sense sulking about it. Melody moved to start the truck, reminding herself she'd been in a worse situation last winter battling her ex-husband for a divorce and always looking over her shoulder.

Only the truck didn't turn over, and Melody leaned forward, half wondering if her dazed state had her doing it wrong. She turned the key in the ignition once more and was met with a cranking sound as the engine tried and failed to start up.

Melody turned and looked wildly to the employee parking lot, seeing Hal's taillights pulling around the corner. Judy was already gone. It was too cold. They worked too hard. They didn't hesitate to rush home.

"No no no!" Melody leaped out of her truck, hoping to catch them before they turned onto the main road.

Her sneakers crunched in the snow, getting wet and soaked as she sprinted out of the well-shoveled parking lot and into the snowbanks. She waved her arms, calling out to Hal, but it was no use. She couldn't catch him. Legs near frozen, lungs burning, face on fire, Melody started crying.

She was tired and lonely and she missed Clay. Life was officially too hard, and she didn't want to play anymore. As childish as it was, she was ready to sit there on the slushy asphalt and sob. She was sick of looking on the bright side, and she was *really* sick of being broke.

With all her heart, she wished Justin would meet with an accident and die a horrible death for doing this to her. For what had to be the millionth time, she kicked herself for marrying him. Melody had never trusted Justin, not really, but her mother had been adamant. He was new in town, a regional manager at a big-name supermarket Melody worked at. He became obsessed with her almost instantly, and Melody's mother couldn't have been more thrilled. Justin was going somewhere. He could change their lives. They could finally stop struggling, but Melody resisted his advances until her daddy got sick. Then she would have done anything to make his last days a little nicer, and they were.

Justin was wonderful. He was supportive and helpful and a total gentleman. He helped fill out forms and paperwork that made Melody's mind swim. He got her father the care he needed. He even helped pay for the more expensive nursing home rather than let her father spend his last days in the one provided by the government. He took Melody and her mother out to lunch a couple of times a week because he insisted they needed to get out and stop working so hard.

After a year of the nice treatment, Melody started to believe she was in love with him. It never felt totally right. It certainly never felt like it did with Clay, but she believed she felt something for Justin as he'd held her close while she'd stood there sobbing over her father's casket.

So she married him.

And that's when it all went to hell.

The company gave him a promotion, moving them to Columbus. He loved the big city and hated the small town where Melody had grown up. Free from the prying eyes of Blue Springs, a town much like Garnet, where everyone knew what everyone else was doing, Justin started to get mean. A bad day at work would lead to arguments, and then the arguments started to end with hitting. Not bad at first, but it escalated over the five years they were married, and Melody found herself oddly desensitized to the abuse because of the steady buildup. The rise was gradual enough, the overwhelming misery a slow burn. She was alone in their big house. She had no friends. She wasn't capable of fitting in with the crowds Justin hung around with.

She had no car to escape, if even for a little while, from the unhappiness. Justin always drove. He controlled everything, and Melody stopped complaining about it rather than fight. When Justin was content, he left her alone. Her life became centered on making him happy, keeping his temper even-keeled and unruffled. She fucked him because the sex made him less combative. She cooked for him because when he was fed, he was lazy. She lived in abject terror that someone or something would set him off. Which it always did, at least a couple times a week, no matter how hard she worked at avoiding it.

It wasn't until she faced the problem of hiding bruises that Melody started to notice many women who've never been in an abusive relationship could be very verbal about spousal abuse. The target of their animosity was always the wife stupid enough to stick around. These women hadn't lived Melody's life. They couldn't understand the conditioning. They didn't experience the strange survival instinct that kicked in and forced her to bend to Justin's will to stay alive and unharmed another day. They'd never felt alone and isolated and afraid of the judgment of others.

Melody knew if she exposed herself as a victim, that's exactly what she would get.

And she was right.

Justin had taken her to the gynecologist to figure out why she couldn't get pregnant. Much to her relief, they'd refused to let him into the room during the exam. The second she was alone, she'd begged for a refill on the birth control pills she'd been taking in secret. Justin had wanted a baby badly. He wanted Melody tied to him by blood and flesh, but there was no way she was going to bring a baby into the mess. She'd kill herself first.

Shocked by her adamancy for contraception, the nurse had asked if her husband hit her, and Melody confirmed he hit her all the time. She'd said it because she wanted to admit it to someone. She'd needed to hear herself air the shame out loud, and she'd *really* needed to make sure she got those birth control pills...

* * * *

The young nurse gave her a stunned look and then asked, "Why didn't you just walk out when he started hurting you?"

Judgment.

It was predictable, and Melody was a little too scarred at that point to care. When the next words out of the woman's mouth were, "I would never—" Melody hopped off the table, heedless of the blue paper gown and cover. She tossed both aside and started getting dressed.

"Wait, you can't leave." She reached out to stop Melody's hasty escape.

Melody jerked her arm from the nurse's grasp. "Can I get my pills or not?"

"There are protocols. I think we have to call the police. I know there are rules to be followed. Doctor Morrow knows what to do. Get dressed and I'll get her."

The nurse ran out of the room, obviously unnerved by Melody's anger. She seemed frightened, as if she were about to get into trouble, which was odd...

* * * *

Little did Melody know that telling a doctor—or a nurse, apparently—you were a victim of abuse started a whole chain of events that ended with Melody living in an abuse center and filing for divorce. She was broke. She was scared. She was friendless and jobless and going through the messiest divorce in the history of the world because Justin didn't want to lose her...but she was free.

The freedom had been so surreally beautiful after what seemed like a lifetime of being caged and afraid, Melody had decided right then she would do anything to hold on to that liberty. When Justin started stalking her after the divorce, Melody began reporting it to the police. When Justin called her, drunk, ranting that it was her fault he'd lost his job because he couldn't survive without her, she called the police.

When Justin tackled her in a parking lot, threatening to kill her if she didn't come back to him, she called the police. Then she packed up and left the small collection of friends she'd made. She said good-bye to the counselors and other women who had slowly gotten used to being beaten and raped and then miraculously got free like Melody had. She left her waitressing job and her dreams of starting her own center for abused women in Ohio and went on a search for a place to call home.

She'd wanted to go back to Blue Springs, but her mother still thought Justin was golden. She believed his stories about Melody being clinically depressed and unstable. Her mother was of the opinion that Melody needed to be medicated so she could go back to her normal, happy life with the perfect husband. The bastard was so charming he'd turned her own mother against her. So she'd looked for something just as good as home, ended up in Garnet, and realized she'd found something *better*.

If fairy godmothers existed, she'd have wished for a do-over tonight. She didn't want a ball or a fancy dress; she just wanted one night with Clay and damn the consequences. It would have been perfect. She instinctively knew they were made to be together. She didn't know how she knew, but she did.

Justin definitely deserved to die for this. He'd ruined her for something amazing, and it wasn't fair. "Bastard," she cursed, letting the anger at her ex-husband bloom because it inspired more self-preservation than sitting and crying. She trudged through the employee parking lot, her shoes sinking into the snow once more as she made her way around the side of the building. If she could make it to the front, she could flag down someone for a jump start. She wasn't going to freeze to death; it just felt like it. "Justin, I hate you! I hate you more than anything! If I had a gun, I'd shoot you myself and I'd enjoy it!"

Cursing out her ex-husband helped her forget about the snow soaking her shoes and her legs being near frozen through her stockings. She made it to the front of the building and paused in shock.

She stared at the streetlamps shining in the customer parking lot. Snow danced like tiny fairies in the beams of light, silhouetting one very expensive SUV that by some unknown miracle was still parked in Clay's usual parking spot.

With tears still streaming down her cheeks, Melody had a wonderful realization: fairy godmothers didn't just exist; they actually granted broken waitresses their wishes!

Chapter Four

Clay sat in his car while Keith Urban played over the radio. He sang a song about breaking up, which was probably the last thing in the world Clay should be listening to. His body was tense with need for Melody. His heart hurt for all the reasons he couldn't have her. A lifetime of avoiding women, and now he'd found one he actually trusted and this happened. Clay would really like twenty minutes in a cage with Melody's bastard of an ex-husband—without gloves.

He silently debated between going to the Cellar and beating on something padded or going home and beating off. He was leaning toward the Cellar, because even if Wyatt was working late, Jules wasn't, and she'd know something was up with Clay the second he walked through the door. Then he'd have to hear advice he didn't have the patience for, and he'd likely say something rude and snappy. Jules would probably punch him for it, which sounded harmless but was actually pretty fucking painful when you considered her running black belt collection. Jules hit low more often than not. All those damn self-defense classes she taught were starting to do away with her sportsmanship.

Yup, the Cellar it was.

What did it matter if he had to wake up in a few hours to train with Wyatt, who would be meaner than usual due to lack of sleep? Good, they could be mean together, because Clay was feeling pretty damn vicious himself. If he wasn't careful, he'd start pretending Wyatt was Melody's fucker of an ex-husband and likely send his best friend to Mercy General. One thing was certain: Wellings was in very big trouble with their upcoming fight, because Clay was ready to kill something.

"Clay!"

Clay pulled himself out of the internal fantasy of beating Melody's ex-husband to death. He frowned through the fogged-up windshield, seeing Melody running through the parking lot. For one brief moment, he thought his mind was playing tricks on him, but he reached for the handle of the door before he could make up his mind if she was real or not.

He jumped out of the car and rushed to meet her, half afraid she'd slip running like she was because the treading on those sneakers had seen better days. Halfway through the parking lot, all he could do was catch her when Melody jumped at him. He wrapped his arms around her, holding her off her feet as she buried her face in the curve of his neck and started sobbing.

"What's wrong?" he asked, fear and concern causing a sickening wave of dread to settle low in his stomach. "Did something happen? Are you hurt?"

"No," she rasped, her breathing labored, her voice heavy with tears. "T-truck wouldn't start."

Clay heaved a sigh of relief, still holding her tightly against him while her entire body shuddered from the cold. Her teeth were chattering against his throat. Her fingers felt like icicles as she slipped them beneath the back of his jacket and underneath his shirt, obviously seeking the warmth of his skin.

"Come on." He turned to walk back to his car, still supporting all her weight as her feet dangled off the ground. "We'll get warmed up, and then we'll get the truck started."

All he heard from her was the *click, click, click* of her teeth chattering, but he didn't need confirmation. He slid into the driver's side of his car, still wearing Melody as a necklace. He reached around her, finding the button to automatically push the seat back. When there was enough room for both of them, he pulled Melody fully into the car and slammed the door shut.

Then he sat there with her on his lap, trying to get his breath back, because he was still recovering from the fear something genuinely terrible had happened to her. He stroked her back soothingly while she pushed her hands deeper beneath his jacket and shirt, her cold fingers splaying over the bare skin of his shoulders.

"I thought I was alone," she finally whispered.

"Nope," he said, infinitely thankful his apprehension about Jules's nosiness and low-hit tactics had left him sitting in the parking lot. "You're not alone."

"I know." She finally lifted her head to look at him. Her glasses had fogged up in the heat of the truck, and she pulled them off, tossing them to the passenger seat. "Thank you."

He nodded, not trusting himself to speak as he stared at Melody curled up in his arms, having never seen her without glasses on. It made her look younger, more innocent. He reached over and caressed her cheeks, flushed pink from the cold. The urge to kiss her was overwhelming.

Melody made the decision for both of them as her hands slid from beneath Clay's shirt to the back of his neck. She tugged him down at the same time she leaned up and pressed her lips against his. The kiss was chaste, soft, and sweet like Melody.

Clay was lost.

It was her scent, flowery shampoo and minty lip balm. It was the feel of her lush body against him. It was the soft sigh of contentment against Clay's lips. He couldn't help but pull her tightly against him and kiss her back, *really kiss her*, pushing his tongue past those full lips and owning her mouth.

He hadn't meant to be quite that aggressive, but Melody responded by clutching at his jacket and parting to his domination, her mouth opening wide to the thrust of his tongue. A low moan reverberated between them and Clay wasn't even sure whose moan it was. It didn't matter, because he was literally drowning in the feel of Melody finally in his arms. Their kissing became hot, openmouthed, and needy as quickly as it had once been soft and sweet.

He fell too fast. His brain shut down under the waves of lust pulsing through his bloodstream. His cock was rock hard, eager, and determined despite the two of them being more than a little exposed in the middle of the diner's well-lit parking lot. He fought the instincts that screamed to push his hands up her skirt and rip at her stockings, searching for something warm and wet to sink his fingers into.

He'd never lost himself this deeply before, and he battled for control, looking for an anchor. Clay forced himself to become aware of the rapid thump of his heartbeat, to notice the rasp of material as they moved against each other. Melody was somehow straddled over him, her fingers in his hair. His UFC cap was gone, probably tossed into the backseat. His hands were underneath her jacket, holding her hips, forcing her tightly against him.

He pulled away from her, because kissing like they were was going to do away with his sanity permanently. He tossed his head back against the headrest as he took a cleansing breath. It did little good because Melody attacked his neck. Her mouth was hot and wet as she nipped and licked and kissed until he was pushing his hips up, his cock straining against the confines of his jeans. He used his hold on her waist to force their lower bodies tightly together, desperately seeking more intimate contact.

"God." Melody's warm breath puffed against the curve of his neck. "I need...I need..." She was panting, sounding as out of her mind and desperate as Clay felt. "I need *you*. Help me."

"Fuck." He groaned, his cock hurting, every muscle in his body tight with the need to give Melody exactly what she was begging for. "We can't."

"Oh no," she sobbed. "No no no."

She didn't give Clay a chance to respond. She used her hold on his hair to tug his mouth back to hers. This time her kiss was anything but chaste. She claimed his mouth as she moved over him in a way that set off every indulgent sensor Clay had.

If Clay didn't care for her as deeply as he did, he would have given in to the tidal wave of lust and just fucked her in the car. He'd never been this hard, this starving for the warm, slick feel of a woman.

"Come on, Mel. Take a breath." He pulled away once more and then reached up to caress the nape of her neck. He tightened his hold just enough to keep her from leaning into him and destroying the last of his self-control. His breathing was rapid and desperate, his voice low and gravelly. "I want this too, okay? I want it more than anything. I'd give up every championship belt I own to be with you, but I don't wanna fuck you in a car. I wanna make love to you in a bed."

"You'll come home with me?" Melody asked, her chest heaving as she sat straddled over him, trying to get her breath back.

"God, yes," he said, a broken laugh slipping out of him. "Can't you feel how fucking hard and desperate I am for you? I'm dying to go home with you. I just sorta, I dunno... I want this to be special, you know?"

"Yeah." She nodded, her green eyes still wild and hungry, but uncertainty spread over her beautiful features. "I want that too, but I don't really know how to make it special."

"Well..." Clay considered that, realizing he had the exact same problem. "I suppose we'll have to try and figure it out, 'cause I don't rightly know how to make it special either. Usually it's just sorta hot and sweaty and uncomfortable."

She laughed, a bright smile making her radiant. "Yeah, that 'bout sums it up."

"But not this time," Clay assured her, knowing that one thing if nothing else.

"No," she agreed, her smile still bright, her dimples carving deep impressions in her rosy cheeks. "Not this time."

"Would it ruin the moment to admit I really wanna get that damn truck of yours fixed before I blow right here?" Clay asked, wincing up at her. "'Cause you're fucking gorgeous over me, and it's sorta messing with my chivalry."

Melody reached up, caressing his cheek. "I think it's sweet."

"There's a first." Clay laughed. "I don't get called sweet too much."

"You should. You're the sweetest guy I know."

Clay rolled his eyes, refraining from mentioning her taste in men could be considered extremely questionable. Instead he helped her crawl off him as they started the shuffle of pulling themselves together. Clay's hat was still missing, but he decided to look for it later. Melody nearly crushed her glasses when she sat in the passenger's seat. Clay pulled his seat up and put the car into drive, forcing himself to stop looking at Melody, because if he stopped long enough to be tempted, they'd never leave this parking lot.

* * * *

Starting the truck was more trying than they'd anticipated, but Clay was motivated and eventually they got it to turn over and start. It felt like a minor miracle when the truck burst to life; the roar of an engine that had seen better days was easily the sweetest sound Melody had heard in a long time.

Clay obviously agreed, because she saw him throw up his hands in triumph. He sat there, gunning the gas for a few minutes before he hopped out of her truck, his breath misty white underneath the headlights. He walked around to the passenger seat and crawled into the car, sitting next to Melody, who'd been pumping the gas pedal while he worked on her truck.

"Okay, you're gonna drive my car back to your place, and I'll follow you in the truck," he announced as he pulled the door closed.

Melody frowned. "Why am I gonna drive your car?"

"'Cause I don't trust the truck," he said, giving her a look. "And it's fucking cold as hell in that piece of shit. We're getting the battery replaced *and* the heat fixed tomorrow."

"Clay—"

"I ain't arguing 'bout it," Clay said in a gruff voice. "We're getting it done, and I don't give a shit if your pride's smarting over it."

Melody huffed but kept her mouth shut. She didn't want to argue with him, not tonight, when she was going to forget every bad thing that ever happened to her and just let this handsome, wonderful man make her feel good.

Her body was humming with yearning and anticipation. She didn't know why everything seemed to click with Clay when she shouldn't click with anyone, but she wasn't going to question good fortune. If whatever compatibility that naturally blossomed between them allowed her to let down her guard and enjoy really being a woman, then she was going to seize the moment before life showed up and ruined it.

He reached out, squeezing her hand in his, his fingers icy. "I'm gonna follow you."

Melody nodded her acceptance and reached down, trying to put the seat up, because Clay was so tall she could barely touch the pedals. She felt underneath the seat, finding nothing helpful. "This car's too fancy for me."

"There's a button."

"I don't see no button, Clay."

"It's there."

"Why can't they just put a darn lever like every other car?"

Clay laughed and then leaned over, his large body draping across hers as he reached down to do it for her. He found the magic button easily, and the seat started to move up on its own accord. When she was close enough to the steering wheel, he bent lower over her lap and kissed her thigh through her thick stockings.

Her breath caught as she looked down at him, that one simple action causing a pulse of pleasure to zing through her body. He caressed her bare upper thigh, pushing her apron and skirt higher up, and then lifted his gaze to hers. Her pussy throbbed to the rhythm of her rapid heartbeat, begging for attention, and it must have been obvious. His dark eyes were sultry, telling Melody he knew without feeling that she was wet and aching for him.

Clay licked his lips slowly, the action looking like a promise with his seductive gaze still holding her captive.

Melody actually squirmed in her seat.

"Let's get outta here." Clay sat up once more, leaving Melody feeling bereft. "Or I'm gonna put my mouth on you right here. I've been fantasizing 'bout tasting you since Thanksgiving."

Melody's eyebrows rose at his boldness. He just blurted out whatever sexual thoughts came to mind, and she found herself really liking the habit. But she couldn't help but admit, "I haven't... I mean, no one's ever, you know...done that...to me."

At first Clay's eyes flashed angrily, as if the admission really pissed him off. But just as quickly his gaze softened, and he reached out to cup her face. "You know what?"

She bit her lip, her cheeks hot. "What?"

"Good." His thumb swept over her bottom lip, his dark eyes studying her face, making her feel as if all her secrets were laid bare to him. "I wanna be your first."

"Well, you ain't gonna be my first," she warned him. "Unfortunately."

"First that counts," he amended, giving her a smile. "And you'll be mine too. It'll be a first for both of us."

"Yeah?" she asked, unable to help returning his smile.

"Oh yeah." Clay pulled away, looking like the action was hurting him. He opened the door without saying good-bye. "Drive careful. I'll be behind ya."

The roads were icy. Melody didn't have a choice but to drive slow and careful, especially when she was driving a car she wasn't used to. There was an insistent throb between her legs that made her want to stomp her foot on the gas, but she behaved. She even drove a few miles under the speed limit while constantly checking to see if the headlights to her truck were still reflecting in the rearview mirror.

The drive felt like forever, but the clock on the dash told her it was less than ten minutes. Melody pulled into the driveway of the small cottage she was renting and got out of the car. She looked at his key chain as she closed the door, finding the button that locked the door. She pushed it, and it beeped back at her.

Melody turned to Clay, who was walking up from where he'd parked her truck. "Is that the right one?"

"That's it." Clay stopped in front of her, staring up at the cottage with a smile quirking at the corners of his mouth. "You put up lights?"

"Yeah, I'm a sucker for colored lights." Melody gave him a guilty smile and turned to walk to the front door because it was way too cold to stand out there a second more than necessary. "The neighbors were throwing 'em away, and I asked if I could have 'em. They had boxes and boxes; most just needed a few replacement bulbs."

"Festive." Clay followed after Melody and handed her keys back. "When'd you find time to put 'em up?"

"Here and there. I needed something to spruce the place up." Melody unlocked the door and held it open for Clay. "It's still sorta empty. I just got what it came with."

Clay stomped his feet on the mat, looking near frozen from the drive. He shivered as he walked in, his arms crossed over his broad chest. "Dang, it's still cold."

"I keep the heat low when I'm gone to save money." Melody flipped on the lights and then walked over to the heater and turned it up. "There ain't much space to heat. I usually take a shower while it's warming up."

"Okay." Clay turned from his sweeping gaze of her living room to give Melody a hot look. "Sounds like a plan to me."

Melody considered him for one long moment. Normally she would pull away, but damn it, this was her wish and her night and she didn't hesitate. "Then okay. Let's take a shower while the heat kicks in."

She walked into the bedroom and flipped on the switch blindly, then worked on the zipper of her jacket. Despite the longing, she was anxious. It felt wrong to seize the moment like this. She didn't know if she'd be this open to letting a man love her tomorrow, but she sure needed it tonight, nerves or not.

Her hands shook in a way that had nothing to do with the cold as she pulled down the zipper to her jacket, feeling exposed. "Clay—"

He stepped into her personal space before she could complain, cupping a hand at the back of her neck and kissing her. She was nervous, but she couldn't help but part to him, warmth dancing over her skin as his tongue pushed past her lips. She clutched at his arms, digging her fingers into the material of his jacket.

She stood on her toes to kiss him more fully, because he was one seriously tall man. Six-five, two hundred sixty pounds of muscles made her bedroom look decidedly smaller when Clay was filling up the space. For the first time since she'd moved in, the house felt comforting to be in, and she clung to the feeling, needing it desperately. She ached and yearned and grasped frantically for more of that warm, safe feeling that always blossomed whenever Clay was near.

Then Clay moaned, suddenly pushing away from her with a scowl. "I forgot to stop by the drugstore."

"That's okay; I'm on the pill. I ain't been with anyone since Justin, and I've been tested since him," she assured Clay, her breath already a rapid pant of desire.

"I gotta get tested before every fight. I know I'm clean," Clay said, his breathing as shallow as hers. "Is this really okay?"

"I think so." She nodded, feeling like she'd die if it wasn't. "I think it's fine. Kiss me again."

Clay didn't need to be told twice. He kissed her once more, thrusting his tongue past her lips to explore her mouth. He tugged at her jacket, pushing it off her shoulders to land on the floor. His hands glided from her hips, up to her bare arms, which were already prickling with goose bumps. His thumbs grazed the sides of her breasts as he rubbed his rough palms swiftly over her chilled arms, trying to warm them up.

It might have worked if his fingers weren't still half-frozen from the ride home.

"Shower," he whispered against her lips.

Melody couldn't argue with that reasoning. They were both freezing. She went to the bathroom and turned on the shower, letting the steam rise up out of the stall. Every night she let the water run for a few minutes, hoping to take the cold out of the ceramic tiles.

It was a few degrees too chilly to make getting undressed sexy. With the bathroom door shut, the two of them pulled off their clothes and shoes hastily. Melody didn't allow herself the luxury of really appreciating Clay naked as all that wonderful male flesh started to be revealed. Clay jerked his shirt off quickly, showing off a thin dusting of black hair over his broad, muscular chest, and flung the long-sleeved shirt into a growing pile with their shoes, socks, and other clothes.

Melody did the same, tossing aside her apron and blue uniform, deciding it could stay on the floor when usually she made a point to wash it before bed. She worked on her stockings and sensible bra and panties, happy to get them off because they weren't anything special on the eyes.

She tried not to think about the fifteen pounds she could afford to lose or the tiny white lines that showed on her hips. She just pulled open the door and jumped into the shower. Clay did the same, crowding in behind her and closing the frosted door, his huge frame taking up most of the space in the stall.

"Ain't you ever heard of bath mats?" Clay asked.

"They're on the list," Melody said, turning her back to him as she worked on undoing her hair.

Clay's big body blocked the stream of water, which was fine because it'd likely sting with how cold she was. She let the hot mist warm her up as she set each pin she pulled out of her hair on the ledge next to the shampoo. She could feel Clay's gaze on her now, the warm water doing away with his haste and complaints.

The tension was strangely palpable weighing heavy in the air as it mixed with the wet steam. She could hear Clay's breathing over the thrum of the shower—shallow, hungry, like that of a wild animal. It made Melody's body hum while she worked on taking out the last of the bobby pins keeping her hair up in the tight bun she needed for work.

Was she really showering with this man? Weren't the two of them doing it backward? She was certain normal people had sex first and then moved on to the couple intimacies like showering together and brushing their teeth side by side.

Suddenly Clay touched the small of her back, his large palm resting against the curve of it. The gentle contact made her jump from the shock of pleasure. The first touch felt like the strike of a flint that ignited an inferno of desire. She froze under the surge of passion, a deer in the headlights. Her pussy clenched; her clit throbbed with a pulse of need that matched the heartbeat pounding in her ears.

Her hair tumbled down her back—too heavy to stay where it was without the pins to hold it. Clay gasped in response, his large body leaning into hers as he bent down and buried his face in the thick, wheat-colored strands now sticking to her wet shoulders and back.

Clay broke the silence with a low rasp of appreciation, his face still tucked into the curve of her neck as he breathed deeply. "I like your hair down."

She couldn't help but arch into him, the feeling of his wet skin against hers making the pounding lust impossible to deny. "I need to get it cut. Been lazy 'bout it."

"Don't you dare." Clay pulled her hair aside, looking for bare skin and finding it as he placed a kiss against the tender spot behind her ear. "I think it's sexy. I think you're sexy."

He pushed his hips against her, his hard cock sliding up the curve of her back. Melody squeezed her eyes shut against the electric shock of pleasure that sizzled through her, making all the tiny hairs on her arms stand on end. She was half hoping he'd just turn her around and fuck her against the shower wall. Lord knew he was certainly big enough to support her.

She lost herself in the erotic fantasies fueled by the feel of him pressed against her, his breath warm against the curve of her neck. His hand slid over her thigh, caressing the silky length of it before he cupped her ass possessively.

"Please." She breathed heavily, not knowing what she was begging for but feeling like she'd die if she didn't find it. "Help me."

She hadn't expected to burn this hot this quickly. She grabbed his hand and brought it to her breast, looking for some sort of release from the building tension. He palmed it, his thumb brushing over her nipple, making Melody gasp out loud. The pleasure zinged straight to her pussy, and her hips jerked forward. She felt starved with yearning and empty without him. She didn't really know how to tell him what she needed when she wasn't sure herself. She'd never ached like this before.

Clay's other hand tangled in her hair, tugging her head back. He captured her lips, forcing her to swallow his low groan. It was then Melody sensed how tense he was, feeling his hands shake as they ran over her body as if desperate to memorize her. He was needy too; he was just better at hiding it.

Melody turned in his arms, both of them gasping at the feel of her breasts pressing against his thick, muscular chest. The pleasure of being in his arms was molten, electrifying every cell in her body because it felt so good to be skin to skin with him.

Their lips met once more, their connection magnetic and mysterious. Melody tangled her fingers in his wet hair, clinging to it like a lifeline as their tongues brushed. Clay was so hard, so strong. His presence both soothed and inflamed when he was clothed; now naked and shaking with need in her arms, her want for him was totally overwhelming.

"Please," she begged once more, the two of them still sharing the same air as she stood on her toes to savor more of his bare skin against hers.

Clay panted with her, his breath warm against her lips, his dark eyes dazed and hungry as he studied her face. "But—"

"It's special," Melody promised as she let go of his hair only to stroke his bare chest, relishing the feel of cut muscles shifting under her fingers. Her touch moved to his upper arm to clutch at his massive bicep. His raw strength was awe inspiring and sexy. She closed her eyes at the thought since it was making the throb between her legs too painful to be denied. "It's special, Clay. It's special because it's with you. It'd be special anywhere."

Clay gripped her hips, and Melody expected him to push her away like he had in the car. Instead she choked back a gasp when he lifted her up. He pushed her against the shower wall, the tiles cold against her bare back, but what did she care? Clay was kissing her again, his thick, hard cock pressing against her pussy, which clenched to feel more of him.

Having a man this close, practically inside her, was different than she remembered. He seemed too big. She wished she could reach down and feel him. She wanted to stroke the full length of that thick cock nudging at her opening, but all she could do was hold on to him while his tongue owned her mouth. She twined her arms around his neck as their lips met over and over again. Their kissing was carnal and passionate in a way she'd never imagined. Sharing the same air with him was addictive. Connecting with him tasted like her first sip of wine—sweet and intoxicating. She wanted *more*.

She writhed, shifting her hips up until the head of his cock brushed her throbbing clit. She never got more than a small taste of heaven because he was holding her in a way that sapped her control. His arms were hooked under her knees, opening her wide, leaving her exposed and waiting for that first hard thrust that never came. Instead the crescendo built; the need boiled and raged. Melody would be begging if she could give up the addictive feel of his kiss long enough to find her voice.

Finally it was Clay who voiced the agony of denial. His breathing labored and shallow, he groaned. "I can't...I can't wait, Mel."

"Then don't." Melody panted, the two of them still sharing the same air. One breath, one heartbeat. "Fuck me."

Clay's forehead fell to hers. His gaze held her captive as he studied her. She could see the defeat in him, an ultimate surrender to the overwhelming passion that exploded between them. It showed on his handsome face before his eyes closed, and he slowly lowered her onto his cock. A shocked gasp tore out of Melody from the bolt of pleasure that came from the first push of the head inside her. He was so big he stretched her almost painfully, but her pussy was wet and needy for him, quivering to be taken. She bowed to the ecstasy, submitting herself to the thrust of his hips against hers. She savored the leisurely slide of being stretched and filled until his thick cock topped out, nudging her cervix and halting his claiming of her.

"Fuck," Clay growled, his fingers digging into the small of her back as her legs remained hooked over his elbows. His body shook, and he shifted his hips against hers, as if trying to get deeper, but he was too big. "Gimme a minute, 'cause I'm gonna lose it. You feel so good, so tight. Christ, I feel like I'm fucking dying."

Melody nodded wordlessly, understanding his mindless desperation.

She lowered her head, still trying to breathe past the ecstasy that didn't want to yield to the stillness and sacredness of the moment. She searched for something carnal, something flesh and bone to distract her from the emotional current of synchronicity pulsing in the air around them.

She stared down at Clay's cock, wet with her juices, stretching her tightly and buried deep. The soft pinkness of her sex wrapped around the thick, steely length of Clay's cock. It was an oddly beautiful picture because it was the two of them together. Bodies joining shouldn't be such an erotic sight, but it was and she was forced to close her eyes against it. Seeing the visible evidence of their connection was going to push her over the edge.

She tossed her head back against the tiles and arched her back to the throb of pleasure ricocheting between them. With a low growl of hunger, Clay lost his battle for control. He pulled out of her gently, only to thrust back in hard and fast. The contradiction was shocking, the pleasure even more so. The sear of bliss was so sweeping it stole Melody's breath, but she had no choice but to weather the storm.

Clay started fucking her hard, using the elbows hooked under her legs to keep her open to each thrust. Melody tightened her hold on him, tangling her fingers in his hair. She forced his mouth back to hers, their kisses frenzied as Clay fucked her, and Melody reveled in the claiming. Teeth clashing, tongues brushing, their low moans evaporated to shallow pants of pleasure as the tide rose.

Melody didn't even have a chance to be stunned; all she could do was give in to the fierce race to completion. Pressed hard against the shower tiles, open wide to the thick, swift slide of Clay's cock in and out of her, every demanding thrust pushed her closer to oblivion. Finally it was too much. The fall was swift, powerful, and all-consuming. She trembled and cried out. Awash in bliss, she managed to reach a pinnacle with Clay she'd only found on her own before.

Shaking in his arms as wave after wave of ecstasy pulsed through her system, Melody jerked Clay down with her. His thrusts became faster, more erratic before he stiffened in her arms and shuddered from the force of his climax. Then they were lost in the same sea, coasting on the same tide.

Melody wanted to stay in this moment forever, with Clay's harsh breathing teasing her ear and his massive body wrapped up in hers. Tiny pulses of pleasure radiated from her pussy and flooded into her arms and legs. She could feel the jerk of Clay's cock inside her and knew he was having the same aftershocks. Words were gone, obliterated completely, because they'd both been reduced to trembling wrecks in the aftermath of such furious orgasms.

Weak and sated, Melody's head fell back against the tiles once more, and Clay took the invitation to drag his tongue up the line of her throat. When Melody made a sound of appreciation, he started licking and kissing her neck. His worship was gentle, endearing, and it had her clenching around him because her skin was still extremely sensitive.

When their heartbeats returned to normal and their breathing evened out, Clay nipped her chin and asked, "You okay?"

She gave him a lazy smile. "I'm great."

He returned her smile, his chest puffing out with well-deserved male pride. "You wanna get down?"

"No, I wanna stay here forever."

"Me too," he said softly and then winced. "But it'll probably get old real fast."

She shook her head in denial. "Nuh-uh."

Stubborn and bullheaded as usual, he set her down despite her rather colorful complaints against it. It was a good thing he was still holding on to her, because Melody's legs gave out once her feet touched the shower floor. Her thighs ached, her pussy even more so because Clay was certainly built proportionally.

"Ouch," she moaned, still holding on to his big shoulders. "Dang, you're big, Clay. I ain't seen a man as big as you."

"Did I hurt you?" Clay asked quickly, sounding concerned. "I should've gone slower."

"Hush," she snapped at him. "If you say one bad thing 'bout what just happened, I'll smack you."

"Well, we can't have that." Clay laughed despite the concerned scowl still making deep impressions in his forehead. "Still, I should've been more gentle."

"I liked it rough," she promised him, waggling her eyebrows to prove her point. "So stop complaining. I think I can feel my feet now."

She thought that would be enough to have him letting go of her, but Melody realized if she wanted to get clean, she was going to have to do it with Clay still holding on to her. So she grabbed the bath scrunchie and body wash and started washing up.

"You ain't got any real soap in this shower?" Clay asked, his big body draped over hers, his arms wrapped around her waist from behind as she worked at scrubbing her arms. "I can't go to the Cellar tomorrow smelling fruity. Wyatt'll never let me hear the end of it. You know how he yaps."

Melody giggled, her body still pleasantly humming from the aftermath of their encounter. She held up the bath scrunchie for him to smell. "It's cucumber melon."

"Oh, that makes it better," Clay said drily. "Last I checked, melons were fruit."

"But cucumber's unisex. I think you'll smell nice."

Clay buried his face in the curve of her neck, hiding under Melody's long, wet hair, which clung to her neck and shoulders. He grabbed the scrunchie from her and took over the task of washing. Melody leaned back against him. Her eyes closed to the feel of his large, soapy hands sliding over her skin, thinking it was really nice to have someone she trusted enough to take care of her.

* * * *

Melody looked amazing wearing Christmas lights.

Clay stared at her spread out on the bed, skin still dewy from the shower, wet hair hiding full breasts and pink nipples. The blink from the lights shining in through the windows reflected off her pale skin in the near darkness of the room, dancing in colored shadows over her lush body. He was mesmerized by her, so beautiful and open and willing for him.

The cynical side of him was screaming to be careful. Nothing felt this good without repercussions, but Clay made a firm decision to ignore his cynical side, not just for Melody, but for himself too, because he wanted this—wanted her.

"What're you staring at?" Melody asked, giving him a bemused smile as she looked up at him hovering over her.

The rush of emotion he felt for this woman scared the shit out of him, but he couldn't seem to stop the fall. Rather than admit he was memorizing everything about her spread out and waiting for him to make love to her, he just shrugged and bent down. He captured one pink nipple with his mouth, lightly tugging on it with his teeth. Melody moaned and arched into him. Her fingers tangled in his hair, holding his mouth to her.

Already turned on despite the bone-melting orgasm he'd just had, Clay laved his tongue over the taut peak. The shower had been fast and frantic, a necessary release from the build of sexual tension that exploded between them. Now he could touch and tease until she was flushed and sweaty and completely mindless. He pushed his hips against the mattress at the thought of her wild and desperate for him. His cock was already hard and straining against the comforter.

Clay moved to the other breast. He sucked on the tip once more, savoring her low hum of pleasure. He liked the sounds she made. She was surprisingly receptive and uninhibited, but then so was Clay when they were together. He felt cracked open and exposed to her, but he craved her so damn much he couldn't stop to worry about it.

All he could do was give in to the hunger.

Clay moved his lips lower, over the smooth plane of her stomach. He reached down, pushing her thighs apart, forcing her to accommodate the width of his shoulders as he nipped her hip bone.

"Clay," she complained, finally sounding apprehensive. "I don't—"

He rubbed his fingers over her clit, making Melody gasp and curve to his touch. He watched her face, seeing her white teeth sink into a full bottom lip. He kept his touch featherlight, just enough to make her ache for more. He wasn't surprised when her eyes glazed over, emerald green reflecting unrestrained want back at him.

While holding her gaze, he stopped touching her, only to bring his fingers to his mouth. He sucked on two, wetting them, his cock jerking at her taste. Then he reached down, sliding his spit-slicked fingers to her pussy, which was tight and sweet and pink, with only a small, thin line of honey-colored hair trying to hide it from his greedy gaze.

"Are you sore?" he asked in concern, tracing the outer lips of her pussy, which seemed a little too pink and swollen. "Did I hurt you?"

Melody writhed, ignoring his concern, her legs spreading wider, her feet pushing down the comforter as she strained for more of his touch. When he continued to tease, simply running his fingers on the outside of her pussy but not entering her, Melody let out a sob of frustration. "Clay!"

"Tell me if you're hurt," he pressed, wanting to know how gentle he needed to be.

"No," she gasped impatiently. "Now stop teasing."

"Oh, but I like teasing," he couldn't help but admit, admiring how beautiful she was, squirming and flushed for more. "And you get wound up so easily. You're sorta naughty, Mel."

"Only for you," she moaned, opening her eyes to give him a look of consummate pleading. "I dunno why I'm like this with you, but I am and I can't seem to help it."

"You're beautiful like this, didja know that?" he asked, his voice low and husky without his permission. "You look like a fallen angel, spread out and begging like you are right now."

Melody's eyes closed at his words. She hummed once more and gave herself over to his vision of a wanton angel. Sweet and dirty at the same time, she let him tease until a fresh sheen of sweat covered her body and her pale skin became flushed underneath the Christmas lights. He watched her get wet for more, saw her pussy swell with need. When he brushed his thumb against her clit, she nearly came off the bed.

He slid his fingers into her, savoring her keening cry of pleasure as he pushed them into her ripe pussy and then curved them upward. Melody actually screamed, her hands fisting in the comforter, her body vibrating under his touch. He stroked and stretched, making her head toss on the pillow, and that's when he leaned down and sucked on her clit, knowing she was too far gone to complain.

He savored the tang of her sex, licking and sucking on her clit, making tiny sobs of pleasure burst out of Melody as she strained for release. It didn't take her long to find it. Her body quaked when she fell over the edge. Her moans were low and surrendering, and she freed the comforter only to hold his head to her while she rode out the tempest.

Her pussy clenched around his fingers to the pulse of her climax, and his cock jerked in response, aching for her. Hearing her come undone so completely did away with the last of his restraint. He didn't even give her a chance to catch her breath. He surged forward, draped himself over Melody, savoring her soft curves. He hesitated to kiss her, not knowing if she'd take issue, but before he could ask, her fingers were in his hair once more. She tugged him down until they were sharing the same air and her tongue darted out, licking his lips, tasting herself on him.

Holy shit, that's sexy!

If Clay didn't fuck her, he was going to come all over her stomach, because this woman pushed all his buttons and turned him on in ways he hadn't thought were possible. Karma was an asshole. Now he was the one shaking and desperate. His balls throbbed with the need to spill inside her. He lost all semblance of who he was, his vision narrowing to the simple, primal goal of claiming Melody and fucking her until they were both sated and spent.

Clay moaned into her mouth when she kissed him, her tongue pushing past his lips boldly. It made the need burn brighter. He thrust against her, blindly seeking a cure for the tension, his rock-hard cock sliding against silky skin. He would have asked, but he didn't have to. Melody spread her legs wide to his need, wrapping them around his hips, her ankles hooking at his lower back.

With her tongue still claiming his mouth, Clay found heaven for a second time that evening. He slid into Melody, feeling her tight heat envelop him in bliss. He wanted to go slow, to take his time and savor her, but once wasn't near enough to slake the pounding lust that sizzled between them. He wasn't sure if a lifetime would appease the hunger that left him shaking with the rush of ecstasy that flooded his bloodstream as he buried his cock fully inside her.

Melody was shaking too, her hips pushing against his as she squirmed for more. Her kisses became low moans that reverberated through him, making him greedy and heedless of being gentle. He pulled out and thrust back in, this time hard enough to make Melody gasp from the force of it.

Clay couldn't stop.

All he could do was move. He slammed his hips against hers, the slap of skin against skin blending with their moans and pants of pleasure. His palms were splayed wide on the comforter, his thighs straining from the force of his thrusts as Melody clung to his shoulders, her legs still wrapped tightly around him.

He might have tried to find sanity if Melody wasn't wild right along with him. Every thrust had her crying out, "Please please please," as her nails dug into his skin.

The coil just wound tighter, the tension building and building until he was forced to reach down and cup her ass. He clutched the soft, round globe, holding her tighter against him, angling her hips for that next hard plunge. They both shattered, their bodies tensing at the same time, their cries serendipitous and perfect because if he was going to be this lost, he wanted to be lost with Melody.

Clay's cock pulsed as he coated her pussy with his cum. The pleasure of it left him suspended in time as Melody's body clenched around him. Even their climaxes felt in sync, like the beat of their hearts were meant to throb together.

The bliss felt like forever, which was more than enough time to steal his breath and energy in the aftermath. Clay's arms shook in an effort to hold himself up and eventually gave out. He fell on top of Melody, who grunted under his weight. Knowing it was too much, he reluctantly rolled off her.

Clay lay there trying to catch his breath, his heart beating the hell out of his ribs. Recovery took longer than he wanted to wait to touch Melody. He reached out, wrapped his fingers around her upper arm, and tugged gently until she turned and draped herself over him.

"Nice." Melody hummed, her cheek resting against his chest. "'M, sleepy."

"Then go to sleep." Clay knew how hard she worked. Rest was precious when she was always working double shifts, and he wanted her to have as much of it as possible. "There ain't nothing stopping ya from closing your eyes."

Melody took the suggestion and snuggled closer to him. Her legs tangled with his. Her cheek rubbed against his chest. Her hand petted and touched for a few minutes. It didn't take her long to fall lax over him, her breathing evening out to the gentle rhythm of deep sleep. Clay was right there with her. Surrendering himself to the heaviness of gratified exhaustion was easy. He fell asleep, happy and sated, with Melody curled up in his arms.

Chapter Five

Melody woke up slowly, which was nice. No blaring alarm clock, no stumbling exhaustion while she tried to get ready without falling asleep standing up. She savored the gentle rise to full alertness, her body still contented from the night before if not a little sore.

She rolled over, grabbing the pillow Clay had slept on, searching for his scent. It actually smelled disappointingly familiar, but she could pretend he hadn't used her shampoo and body wash in the shower. She thought she smelled him underneath her bath products, and her eyes drifted closed once more.

She wasn't disheartened to be alone. She knew Clay got up before the chickens to train. She wasn't real sure *why*, but she was expecting it. That bouncing out of bed business was not for her. If she didn't have to get up before noon, she wouldn't. She didn't have that inborn need to be productive before the sun rose, but Clay did.

How country was that?

She really wanted to go back to sleep and drift on waves of erotic dreams that were obviously an aftereffect of the mind-blowing evening with Clay, but real life started to intrude. She remembered her uniform still on the bathroom floor that needed to be washed before work. She'd have to get up now if she wanted it to be dry in time.

Her progress of getting out of bed and getting moving was leisurely, which was a nice treat all by itself. She tossed her uniform in the wash first thing, but then she stood by the kitchen counter in her bathrobe and fuzzy pink slippers sipping a cup of sludgelike instant coffee.

She was definitely asking Santa for a coffeemaker this Christmas.

Melody was still sipping her terrible instant coffee—the burn of it waking her up more than anything—when a knock sounded on the door. She set her coffee down and frowned, not expecting anyone. She was hoping it was Clay, but her past made her cautious.

"Who is it?" she called out when she got to the front door, knowing she needed a peephole.

"I have some documents for Mrs. Andrews."

Melody stared at the door, an icy cold wash of fear swamping her system. The shock of it stole her breath. The fall from peaceful to terrified happened between one heartbeat and the next. It took her a few seconds to get acclimated. She'd gotten too comfortable with Clay, too used to feeling safe. She wasn't accustomed to the terror anymore.

"Ma'am?"

"Sorry," Melody said, still trying to get her bearings. She opened the door. It probably wasn't the safest idea, but the reality was Justin wouldn't have paid someone to grab her and then used her married name. He was craftier than that. She found a clean-cut young man bundled up against the cold, a clipboard in one hand and a thick manila envelope in the other. She pulled a face as she eyed him. "What sorta paperwork is it?"

He shrugged, looking irritated and desensitized by his job. He handed her the clipboard, and Melody signed for whatever he was delivering.

He handed her a package. "Enjoy your summons."

"Summons." Melody gasped, hating that roiling swell of fear still churning in her stomach. "What am I being summoned for?"

Package delivered, he obviously didn't have to answer her question. The young man turned around and left her standing in her bathrobe and fuzzy slippers in the open front door. While he walked down her driveway, she tore into the envelope. She pulled out the paperwork, seeing it was some sort of court date for a foreclosure, which would have concerned her if she owned a house, but she didn't. She scanned the legal jargon until she found her name and address listed right underneath Justin's information.

Uncaring of the freezing temperatures and snow-covered driveway, Melody raced after the deliveryman. Her fuzzy slippers were soaked and ice-cold, her robe wasn't doing a very good job of combating the morning chill, but she couldn't feel anything except heart-wrenching terror.

"Did he get one of these?" she called out as she came up on the man crawling into his car. "Did you deliver one of these summons with my address to him?"

"Who's him, lady?" the guy barked, his polite disposition gone now that he wasn't trying to get her to open the door.

"My ex-husband." Melody thrust the paperwork at him and pointed to Justin's name above hers. "Did he get one of these? It's really important that I know if he got one."

"I don't know." He tucked his legs into the car in a silent dismissal of her. "I just do what I'm told, and they told me to drive way the hell out here and give that to you."

"Listen to me," Melody said slowly, the fear making her voice quiver. "If he has my address, I need to know about it because I have a restraining order against him. He wasn't supposed to know where I am. I have no idea how you guys got this address. I don't even know what house this is, but it's really important that you find out if he knows where I am because that means I need to quit my job and move."

The delivery guy looked at her, his gaze running over Melody standing there shivering in the cold in her robe and slippers. "What? You think he's dangerous or something?" he finally asked skeptically.

"Look, I know it sounds ridiculous." Melody sighed, her heart pumping panic through her bloodstream. "I know it seems like I'm just blowing things out of proportion—everyone thinks that—but I'm not. He threatened to kill me, and I'm inclined to believe he's serious. If y'all can find out if he got one these files, I'd really appreciate it."

The guy sighed, his shoulders slumping in defeat. "I guess I could call the office and find out if they were able to locate him."

Melody took a quivering breath, her eyes stinging with tears. "Thank you."

"Just gimme a minute." He reached past her to grab the handle to the car door, his gaze running over her body once more. "Unless you want me to come in and make the calls there?"

Melody looked down at herself, remembering her robe. She'd slipped it on when she woke up, and she was completely bare beneath it. She clutched at the opening that dipped low, her anxiety and suspicion in full gear.

"I'll just go put something else on," she said rather than take him up on the offer. She turned to leave, her cheeks burning. "Just knock."

"Whatever, lady." He huffed, sounding irritated.

Melody raced back up to the house, being careful not to fall. The driveway was covered with only a thin sheen of snow. Someone had shoveled a few hours ago. The yard showed evidence of the night's snowfall. Knowing it was Clay who'd taken the time to do the dreaded task for her, it took more strength than she knew she had not to warm to the idea of depending on him. A part of her was desperate to call the Cuthouse Cellar right now. She wanted Clay near to make her feel safe and secure once more, but this morning showed that letting down her guard left her wide open to being blindsided when the reality of her life came back to slap her in the face.

She locked the door when she was inside and then hurriedly dressed, her fingers shaking as she tried to button her jeans and hook her bra. She should be worrying about getting the hell out of Garnet. Finding a new town was going to be challenging when she had so little saved. She'd lucked into the job at Hal's Diner and the kindness of strangers in Garnet. She couldn't count on it a second time. She'd thought she'd have more time. She'd only set aside a third of her tips when she should have stashed much more than that. But the lack of funds wasn't what was weighing heavily on her mind.

All she could think about was Clay.

She was going to have to leave. She was going to miss him. Worst of all, she was going to hurt him. Tears were running down her face by the time she pulled on a thick sweater and sat on the bed to put on a pair of socks.

A knock reverberated through the house, forcing Melody out of her miserable reflections. She jumped up and dashed to the door. Rather than welcome him in, Melody stepped up next to the deliveryman and closed the door behind her.

"Did you hear anything?"

"They haven't found him," he said simply. "They've been trying at the house listed, but it's always empty. It looks abandoned."

Melody nodded as she tugged nervously at her hair, still hanging loose around her shoulders. "And they don't have any leads?"

"None yet." The guy shrugged. "But we always find 'em eventually. A hospital visit, utilities, cell phone bill—everyone's traceable."

Melody wanted to smack her forehead. The damn utilities—of course she was easy to find. She was officially terrible at being underground—but she was learning.

"Is there any way y'all can call me if you find him?" Melody asked hopefully. "I know that's a big imposition, but I do have the restraining order I can show to your boss. I don't wanna know any of his personal information. I don't care where he is or what he's doing. I just need to know if he gets those papers with my address on them."

"Fine." He looked uncomfortable, like a man who just got dragged into the middle of a nasty argument. "You got a number I can call you at?"

Melody breathed a sigh of relief, knowing this would buy her a little time. She wouldn't have to go into a new town jobless, broke, and living out of her truck like she had been when she got to Garnet. "Thank you."

She turned and went back inside, quickly writing down her home number and the number to Hal's Diner. Melody sat down on the bed after he left, feeling dazed and disoriented from the pain in her chest.

To distract herself, she looked at the papers, discovering she owned a vacation home in South Carolina she never knew about. It should have been shocking, but it wasn't. Justin had ruined her credit years ago. He liked to live above his means. Fancy cars, fancy clothes, and apparently a vacation home in South

Carolina that was likely used during supposed business trips.

The paperwork said he'd bought it four years ago when they were still married. She supposed someone believed she was on board with the purchase, but they didn't know Justin had a collection of false power-of-attorney forms that gave him the authority to do whatever the hell he wanted with her life and her credit. The notaries had just believed his bullshit and signed away her life for a wink and a smile. Justin was a smooth talker and one of those handsome, charming men no one would believe was capable of wrong.

Melody gazed at the papers on the bed, her bottom lip quivering as she thought about the friends she'd made in Garnet and the little cottage she was starting to make a home. She thought about Clay and how perfect and beautiful life felt when they were together. She knew she could never, ever tell him about this because if Justin showed up, Clay would either end up dead or in prison.

Justin was too fixated on owning her.

Clay was too determined to keep her safe.

A fight between them would end with one of them dead, and Melody couldn't bear to think about either scenario. Not because she was particularly fussed over Justin dying; she just didn't want to see Clay's life ruined because of it.

She loved Clay too much to let him get involved in her mess.

Tears streamed down her cheeks, and she buried her face in her hands when the first sob burst out of her. She loved Clay, but she couldn't keep him. To protect both of them she was going to have to disappear in a few weeks with nothing but her memories and her broken heart. She could only hope Clay wouldn't hurt as badly as she was. It felt like someone had thrust a knife into the center of her chest and twisted the blade.

She'd experienced a lot of pain in her thirty-two years. She'd mourned the loss of freedom, passion, and innocence, but not once had she been forced into the horrible position of dropping true love like a hot coal at the very moment she realized it was real and pure.

The loss of it felt like more than she could endure.

Melody had thought it many times before, but this time she knew for sure: life was officially unfair.

* * * *

"You smell *real* pretty."

Clay jammed his elbow back into the center of Wyatt's chest, deliberately using extra strength to prove his point. "Get the fuck off me."

Wyatt wheezed and laughed as he rolled off Clay to lay sprawled out on the mat next to him. Big, broad, and powerfully built, Wyatt's bare chest glistened with sweat as he clutched at it and fought to find his breath. "For getting laid last night...you're sure ornery today."

Clay rolled onto his back and lied. "I didn't get laid last night."

"Right." Wyatt snorted. "You never came home, and you show up today smelling like flowers and strawberries."

"It's cucumber melon," Clay corrected, feeling his cheeks heat. "It's unisex."

Wyatt howled, his hand still splayed over his muscular chest as he rolled on his side and laughed at Clay's expense.

"Ya keep snickering and I'm gonna forget Tony put a stop to cage sparring with you," Clay warned him with a dark scowl. "You wanna spend the day in Mercy General, Sheriff?"

"Bring it on," Wyatt said, his smile still wide and teasing. "I can take you, Powerhouse. I got money riding on this fight. I was throwing the cage fights to keep your confidence up and your brain working regular."

"I thought betting in Garnet was illegal."

"Good thing I got a sheriff in my pocket."

"Are you really betting on the fight?" Clay asked because Wyatt said it often enough he was starting to believe it.

Wyatt gave him a stony-eyed stare, his smile gone. "Maybe."

"That's the same look you use in poker."

Wyatt frowned. "So?"

"You're terrible at poker," Clay reminded him. "Why'd you always say you're betting on the fights when you and me both know you ain't doing any such thing."

Wyatt rolled onto his back and then sprang to his feet, showing off amazing agility and martial arts skill. He ran his fingers through his hair and avoided Clay's eyes as he said, "It's better than saying I'm worried and I don't want you to get too hurt, ain't it?"

Clay considered the confession as he looked up at Wyatt, whose face showed deep concern. Finally he nodded in agreement. "Yeah, that's definitely better. Go back to that; it was working."

Wyatt laughed, his smile bright once more. "Then you better get your ass up and get back to training, 'cause I ain't losing a bunch of money just 'cause you're lazy."

Clay rolled back and then sprang to his feet the same as Wyatt had. Hours of this and he was starting to get tired of the abuse. He didn't want to spar with Wyatt. He wanted to see Melody.

He glanced at his watch and raised his eyebrows thoughtfully. "You wanna take a shower and then go grab lunch?"

"No, I don't," Wyatt said in disbelief. "I had to hire an extra deputy and take a pay cut to be your training partner. Not to mention the night shift I'm on. So guess what, Clay 'Powerhouse' Powers, that's what we're doing. We're gonna train, and you're gonna be fucking happy 'bout it."

"I pay you to be my training partner. You make twice as much off me as you lost in the pay cut."

"Yeah, but I'd be doing it even if you weren't paying me," Wyatt said, giving Clay a look of insult. "Now stop thinking about your *piece of pie* and get your head in the cage before you come back to that pretty waitress in a body bag."

Clay glared, feeling irritated that Wyatt was right. Rather than complain, Clay jumped at him. He threw his shoulder into Wyatt's chest and knocked him off his feet. The two of them started grappling. Fists and kicks were reserved for the equipment after the last cage match that ended with stitches, so all he could do was pin Wyatt enough times to work off the frustration.

* * * *

Muscles aching, freshly showered, Clay was starving and ready for lunch. He put his UFC hat on and walked out of the locker room ahead of Wyatt, who always took longer. Wyatt was going into work after lunch and needed to be in uniform. Plus the asshole was vain as could be. He always fussed with his hair, and the bastard had the nerve to give Clay shit about some cucumber-scented body wash?

"Clay."

He turned around, the smile dying on his lips when he looked at Melody. She was put together for work, with her usual blue and white uniform. Her hair was back up, her glasses on, but her face was flushed, her eyes puffy and red. It was obvious she'd been crying.

Clay rushed to her and instinctively grabbed her waist. He pulled her close, studying her face in concern. "What happened?"

Melody buried her face against his chest rather than look at him. One hand reached up to run over his pectoral muscles, her open palm stopping to rest over the place where his heart was beating wildly out of control.

"Tell me," he pressed, his hand sliding up to rub her back.

She lifted her head, her eyes swimming pools of green beneath her glasses. Her face scrunched up, and she bit her bottom lip against a sob. Clay wanted to push, but he let her take a shuddering breath and waited patiently until Melody finally tilted her head and whispered, "I'm sorry."

"You don't have to be sorry."

She nodded, tears streaming down her face. "Yes, I do."

"What is it?"

"We can't—" She squeaked. Her hand covered her mouth, and her eyes closed tight against the pain that was so palpable Clay could taste it in the air around them. "W-we can't be together anymore."

Clay gaped, his heart plummeting into his stomach. "What?"

"I told you I was broken," she whispered as she lowered her head and wiped at her cheeks. "You should've listened."

"You're not broken, Mel." He rubbed her back again, hoping to God this was just cold feet. He studied her face streaming with tears, red and blotchy; she was still beautiful to him. "I think you're amazing."

"Oh no no no." She shook her head frantically, another sob bursting out of her. "Don't do that. Please don't do that."

"Don't do what?" Clay tried and failed to keep the gruffness out of his voice, because he was suddenly very scared Melody was slipping through his fingers. "What am I doing wrong? Why's this happening?"

"You're being sweet. Please don't be sweet," she begged, her desperation apparent. "It makes it so much harder."

"You don't have to do this," he told her, the wild panic freezing in his chest and settling there like it planned to stay awhile. He gripped her hip harder, pulling her tighter against him. "Whatever this is, we can figure it out."

"No, we can't." She reached into her apron, pulled out a small stack of bills, and pushed it against his chest. "You left this on the nightstand."

"It's yours," he said, feeling his eyes sting in a way they hadn't since he was young and homeless. "I left it for you in case the truck—"

"I know and I appreciate it, but it ain't right." She pushed the money against his chest insistently. "I want you to take it back. I don't deserve it."

"Please take it," he pleaded, his face hurting from the effort it took to hold his emotions. "Take the money. I want you to have it."

She bit her lip and then leaned down, pushing the money into his pocket while he stood there frozen and horrified.

"I wish it could be different." She sighed in a soft, anguished voice that bled with longing. "I wish it more than anything, Clay, and I'm *so* sorry it can't."

"I don't accept this," he snapped because everything about this felt wrong. "Something happened, and I wanna know what it is. I *deserve* to know."

She turned to leave rather than answer him, which only deepened his suspicion. He wasn't just going to sit back and watch her walk out of his life. He reached out and grabbed her arm, not willing to let it go at this. Melody flinched violently in reaction to his hold. Her knees bent; her eyes opened, wide and terrified.

Clay let go of her like he'd been burned, having a horrible realization. "You're scared of me?"

"I'm sorry," she said rather than argue, her face still scrunched up against entirely breaking down. "I have to go now. Please don't request my section at Hal's."

Clay didn't have a choice but to watch her run off. He stood in the back hallway of the Cuthouse Cellar, watching his heart run away from him in a blue and white waitress uniform. It turned out the sound of heartbreak squeaked like sneakers with bad treading sliding against linoleum.

This couldn't be happening.

He hadn't spent a lifetime pushing women away only to be taken down by a piece of pumpkin pie. There was no fucking way this could be his undoing. It felt surreal because he wasn't raging and furious; instead he felt broken and devastated. His pinpoint vision on Melody blurred when she rounded the corner.

He couldn't believe it. Someone or something *not* Melody was doing this to him, because never in a million years was he going to be convinced she wanted this. She'd looked exactly how he felt, like some terrible, malevolent force had just ripped out her heart and stomped on it for good measure.

If he ever got ahold of that force…he'd end it.

The idea of revenge should offer some comfort, but the room was still swimming and gray, making him feel like losing Melody had taken the color out of his life. He'd forgotten who he was before she'd shown up. Bitter and unhappy, with two friends he trusted and a sea of acquaintances who didn't give a fuck about Clay outside his ability to be a meal ticket to anyone good at capitalizing on strength, agility, and violence as a sport.

He was going to sit there and actually *cry* if he didn't find an outlet for the pain and crushing loss trying to swallow him whole.

"You left cash on the nightstand?"

Clay turned his bewildered gaze on Wyatt, who walked over and stood next to him. With his tan, wide-brimmed hat in his hand, Wyatt pulled a face of disappointment.

"I feel like I should arrest you for that. That's pretty darn bad, Clay."

Clay frowned, the shock and heartache making his thinking process fuzzy. "What?"

"No wonder she dumped you," Wyatt went on with a wince. "I knew this was a nightmare waiting to happen. I'm probably gonna have to tell you 'I told you so' once the shock of getting kicked to the curb wears off."

As it happened, an outlet for the pain dressed in a sheriff's uniform and had a tendency to gloat no matter how dire the situation. Clay didn't even hesitate before he raised his fist and nailed Wyatt, savoring the crunch that meant he'd just broken his best friend's nose.

Chapter Six

Clay closed his eyes, letting the hot water hit his face, trying to will away the stress and tension. He hated the buildup before a fight. Living out of hotels. The media blitz. Cameras shoved in his face for training. They thought they were getting a feel of his life as an MMA fighter; what they were actually seeing was a staged show that Clay was an unwilling participant in.

Clay bitched and moaned through the whole process every single time. His coaches yelled, and Clay ignored them. Promoters cried about sponsors and fans while Clay did a pretty good job of not hearing them. His agent took lots and lots of antacid.

Clay didn't want to talk to people. He certainly didn't want to give interviews. He remained steadfast in his determination to be as uncooperative as possible, because this was a fight, not a circus, and the day he started willingly being a clown, he'd quit.

Then Wyatt would come along and somehow talk him into doing a few interviews and nudge him into doing a training camp promo. Clay would give martial arts tips and talk about past fights for the cameras because that seemed moderately worthwhile when you considered the art of Mixed Martial Arts. He'd sign autographs and pose for pictures because it wasn't the fans' fault he was naturally an asshole.

Wyatt would push and Clay would eventually play along just to shut him up, because his yapping could really get on Clay's nerves. That was past fights, where Clay would watch the promotional footage later and realize he'd ended up being a slave to the machine and he'd be disappointed in himself. If there was one small comfort in getting dumped a week before his trip to Las Vegas, it was that no one could accuse him of being a clown this time.

His team gave up the first day they arrived, because the reality was, they were lucky Clay was there to participate in the fight in the first place. Getting him to be a clown for the masses was the least of their concerns. Their angle on Clay's bad attitude changed from bitching at him to get with the program to coaxing and begging him to pull himself together long enough to win. At the very least, they hoped he wouldn't get destroyed by Wellings, who wasn't just hamming it up for the cameras but also looked pretty damn vicious in training.

Everyone, including his own team, was expecting Clay to lose, and Clay couldn't find it in himself to give a fuck about it. He wasn't going to get crushed like they feared. Over twenty years of intense martial arts training was hard to forget. His fighting responses were deeply ingrained. He could fight on autopilot—training with Wyatt since middle school insured that—he just couldn't go the distance.

The fight tomorrow was an issue; Clay knew it on some level. Instead he found himself thinking of

Melody as the hot water beat against his face. He knew something was up. He didn't believe she'd just walked away from what they shared for nothing. She was working harder than before. In the days since she pushed him away, she'd started to lose weight. The dark circles under her eyes were more than exhaustion. Fear and desperation showed on her face, and Clay was frantic because there wasn't a damn thing he could do about it.

He turned off the shower and leaned past the curtain to grab a towel. They had him in one of those outrageously opulent hotel rooms Las Vegas did so well. With marble floors and gold fixtures and way too much space. The bathroom was enormous, with a huge Jacuzzi tub and a separate shower. Melody would have enjoyed this fancy room if she'd agreed to come with him.

* * * *

"Mel."

Melody turned, eyes wide, a fork held halfway to her mouth. She glanced around Clay to the front of the diner, obviously making sure no one saw him come into her workspace. "What're ya doing back here?"

"I know you take a break after the lunch rush to grab a bite," Clay admitted, feeling his cheeks heat over being so obvious about watching her. He rubbed at the back of his neck, looking away from her. "I just...I'm glad you're eating. It looks like you're losing weight."

Melody laughed cynically. "I can afford to lose a few pounds."

"Don't say that." Clay frowned, letting his gaze roam over her. He'd given her space because she'd asked for it, but the separation was killing him. "I miss you, Mel."

Melody squeezed her eyes shut and took a shuddering breath. She bit her lip rather than reply. The pain was written all over her face, sharp and tangible enough to convince Clay staying away wasn't the right card to play. He stepped into her personal space. The magnetic pulse that drew them together flared to life, ricocheting fierce and electric between them. The hair on Clay's arms actually stood on end. It felt like taking his first drink of water after days in the desert. He reached out and grabbed her hand because he needed the connection.

"Oh don't." Melody's eyes swam like lost emeralds behind her glasses when she tilted her head to give Clay a pleading look. "Please don't do this. I'm begging you not to do this."

"Come with me to Vegas tomorrow," he went on, refusing to release his hold on her hand. She didn't pull away, and he got the distinct impression she needed the connection too. "You don't have to watch the fight, but they always dump a bunch of money on fancy hotel rooms, and I know you'll like it. You can see the three-ring circus, cameras and fans and a bunch of bullshit everyone but me seems to think is exciting."

"You don't like it?" Melody asked in concern. "I thought this was your dream."

"I like the art of battle," he admitted with a smirk. "I like fighting. I like the satisfaction of winning, but I hate the circus."

Her smile was sad as she squeezed his hand. "I wish I could go."

"You can," he assured her. "Come with me. Make the bullshit bearable."

"I can't." She pulled her hand out of his, looking like the action was hurting her. She turned back to the food that she'd been standing there eating. She pushed at it halfheartedly with her fork and then whispered, "Please take care of yourself."

Clay knew a dismissal when he heard one, and he had to take a cooling breath in response. He wanted to needle her until she told him what had happened to change everything, but he knew it wouldn't get him anywhere. He was still haunted by the look of fear in Melody's eyes when he'd grabbed her arm outside the locker room.

Words were trapped in his throat, because he wasn't great at expressing himself. He'd never had a girlfriend before. He'd never had anyone to care about except Jules and Wyatt, and the two of them knew as much about the softer emotions in life as he did. He was in foreign territory, but he wanted to find a way to tell her that every minute away from her felt like a small death. These past few days had stretched out like an eternity, and he really didn't see how he could survive a lifetime without her.

Melody was still pushing at her food, two silent tears running down her cheeks until she reached up to hastily brush them away. He should say it. Just give in to instinct and lay every rough sentiment welling up inside of him out in a terrible gush of emotion. He knew it would be dreadful to witness because he was horrible at this stuff. He'd probably say all the wrong things in all the wrong ways, and Melody would likely get every word because she understood him.

He took a deep breath and willed the words to come.

"You okay, darling?"

Clay groaned, turning to see Judy come around the corner. Her eyes were narrowed at the two of them, darting from Melody still silently crying to Clay standing there tense and vibrating with a sea of unfamiliar emotions.

"Fine." Melody nodded, wiping at her cheeks once more. "Clay was just—"

"Leaving," Clay finished for her, because he didn't want her to get in trouble. He reached out and squeezed her small hand once more in his big one. "I'll see ya, Mel."

"See ya." She turned to give him smile. "Good luck."

Clay let go of her hand and turned to leave, feeling anything but lucky...

* * * *

Clay wrapped a towel around his waist and walked out of the bathroom feeling raw and miserable. He winced as he stepped into the large suite. His room was crowded with people, and it reminded him why he'd gone to hide in the second bathroom to begin with. He'd been trying to escape Wyatt, who'd set up camp in Clay's bedroom and hovered like an annoying mother hen.

Jasper and Tony sat at a table in front of the window. The two coaches ignored the impressive skyline of Las Vegas at dusk. Instead they huddled close together, speaking in gruff whispers.

His publicity manager, Eloise, sat on the couch glued to her laptop. Clay saw she was reviewing footage of him training earlier in the afternoon. His agent, Rick, lingered in the marbled foyer of the suite, speaking into his top-of-the-line smartphone. Rick stopped midsentence, whatever he'd been talking about obviously not for Clay's consumption. Instead Rick gave him a big, false smile that churned his stomach.

"Hey, buddy!" Rick's voice was high-pitched in the annoying way it got when he was nervous and trying very hard to hide it. He held up a finger to Clay and then whispered into the phone, "Let me call you back. Clay just got out of the shower."

"You didn't have to do that," Clay said, refraining from adding that he didn't want to talk anyway. "I'm just gonna take a nap."

"Good." Rick gripped Clay's bare upper arm, squeezing the muscle. "Go lie down. Get rested. Wyatt ordered up a massage for you."

Clay pulled a face of distaste. "I don't—"

"It's good for you. It'll relax you, keep you loose for tomorrow."

Clay studied Rick, with his false smile and tense lines around his beady blue eyes. Then he turned to look at everyone else. Jasper had been training him since he was in middle school. Tony showed up when Clay and Wyatt had first started on the MMA circuit. The two of them had showed enough promise in their youth that Tony moved to Garnet and never left. He liked both coaches well enough, but he was officially over bleeding for them and all the other leeches that benefited off his hard work. They were an excellent crew. Clay wouldn't work with people who weren't good at what they did and decent folks to boot, but he still felt done.

"I quit," he told Rick simply. "As soon as I'm done with my contract, I'm retiring."

Rick let out a nervous laugh and patted Clay's bicep once more. "You're just uneasy. It's prefight nerves."

"I'm not nervous," Clay assured him. "Either I win or I lose; I don't really give a shit. I'm done, Rick. I'm not fighting anymore. I've been on the circuit half my life. I'm done with the circus."

"We'll talk after the fight." Rick balled up his fist, doing a fake jab and dodge. He lifted his leg, kicking at Clay's bare shin with his fancy shoes. "You got 'em, right, Powerhouse?"

He shook his head in reaction, feeling like Rick had just spit on a sport that had been a lifestyle and an art form to Clay since he was a kid. "Don't do that."

"I'm getting you pumped." Another fake punch, this time tapping Clay's jaw.

Clay turned and headed for his bedroom, knowing he was about to say or do something he might *not* regret. Didn't these assholes have their own rooms? Why were they all camped out in Clay's suite?

Clay paused at the open door to the bedroom, hearing Wyatt talking in a low voice.

"I'm telling ya, I'm reviewing the video now. Wellings is on his game; ain't no way of denying it. The octagon's fresh for him. He got a first-round knockout two weeks ago. Clay's been underground for months. He's not hungry like Wellings. We're in trouble."

Clay frowned, his pride prickling. He couldn't give a shit about everyone else, but Wyatt losing faith in him hit pretty low below the belt.

"I dunno." Wyatt sighed, jerking Clay back into the conversation. "If he can get him to the mat, he's got a chance. This guy is sprawl and brawl all the way. Clay's taken down plenty of 'em before, but his head's not in the fight. I don't think he gives a shit. There's no fucking drive; he's been training on instinct since—"

Wyatt huffed, making it obvious he'd been interrupted, and then sounded exasperated as he barked, "What the hell am I supposed to do 'bout it, Jules? Don't ya think I'm the last guy in the world who should be coaching him on love? I ain't exactly succeeded at it. Why can't you do something 'bout it? Aren't you naturally supposed to know how to fix this shit due to the parts God gave you?"

There was a long pause before Wyatt groaned. "Christ, please don't start. Okay, fine, you're right, women's liberation, blah, blah, blah. Can't you just, I dunno, lie or something. Tell him his girl's changed his mind, get him through the fight and—"

Clay chose right then to walk in. If he listened to any more, he was going to break Wyatt's nose a second time, and he'd rather not. He'd felt sort of guilty about it the last time. He looked to Wyatt, who still had the green-tinged bruising from the injury across the bridge of his nose and darkened smudges beneath both eyes.

Wyatt winced as he looked up at Clay. "How much did you hear?"

"Enough." Clay scowled. "I ain't gonna get crushed by a cocky bastard like Wellings, so you can stop crying on the phone to Jules and getting her worked up."

"You wanna talk to her?" Wyatt held out the phone with a hopeful look on his face.

"Nah." Clay didn't want to talk to anyone. He wanted to lie down and take a power nap before the weigh-in. "I'm closing my eyes."

Clay walked to the bed and fell facedown on the comforter. He hated everything about where he was at that moment. It was almost hard to believe he used to live and breathe to fight. It hadn't been about the money, though the money was nice. It was about the art of battle and the wild rush of adrenaline that came from being in that cage with nothing but skill, strength, and endurance to help him be victorious. Now it was about getting it over with. Fighting had lost its thrill, and that was a pretty damn good indication it was time to retire.

"I ordered a massage."

"Don't want it," Clay mumbled into the comforter. "Cancel it."

"You're tense. It's obvious."

"Then order me a blowjob."

"Are you serious?" Wyatt asked as if considering it. "'Cause I'm sure that can be arranged. You wouldn't even have to pay for it; there's a whole shitload of groupies who—"

"Fuck off, Conner." Clay reached up and grabbed a pillow. His feet hung off the bed, but he didn't care. "How am I supposed to nap with ya yapping at me?"

"Aren't you gonna talk to Jules?"

"Nope," Clay said simply, wondering why everything needed to be told twice to Wyatt. "Tell her I'll see her tomorrow."

"She'll be running late. You probably won't see her till after the fight."

"So I'll see her after the fight."

Wyatt was quiet for a long moment before he whispered into the silence of the room. "I do have a lot riding on this fight, you know? Both of us do."

Clay huffed in defeat and held out his hand blindly, knowing that was Wyatt's warning that he was about to get sentimental. When Wyatt put the phone in his open palm, he brought it to his ear. "I ain't gonna get killed, and I'm sorta insulted you're believing it."

"I don't believe it," Jules said, sounding honest. "I just wanna make sure your head's in the fight."

"It's not," he replied because lying wasn't one of his strong suits. "But I'm sure I'll hold my own anyhow. I'll see you tomorrow after the fight."

"Fine," Jules grumbled, sounding nervous and exasperated. "And I don't wanna see you all dented and damaged neither. I wanna see you in good condition."

"Fine," Clay agreed and then added, "Bye, Jules. I love you."

Jules paused for a long moment before she whispered, "I love you too, Clay. You're the last family we got. You'll remember it, right? That little waitress ain't the only one worth surviving for, okay?"

"Okay." Clay felt a little warmth seep back into his heart. A thread of life tunneled through the pain. He might be surrounded by leeches who used him as a big, mean paycheck, but there were still two people in the world who saw more than dollar signs when they looked at him. "I got it handled. I'll live to scowl another day."

Jules laughed. "You better."

When Clay hung up, he tossed the phone aside and then tilted his head to glance at Wyatt, who stood there looking worried. He winced as he studied Wyatt's bruised face. He was a yapping, pushy pain in the ass, but he was still Clay's best friend and he loved Wyatt like a brother.

"I'm sorry 'bout your nose."

Wyatt raised surprised eyebrows. That was the first injury Clay had ever apologized for, and there had been *many*. "Are ya getting soft on me, Powers?"

"I dunno." Clay closed his eyes, remembering Melody naked and sprawled out on her bed wearing nothing but Christmas lights. He found himself missing her with every fiber of his being. "Maybe."

"That ain't good." Wyatt sighed. "That ain't good at all."

* * * *

The lunch rush was busier than usual. Melody figured it was Christmas being around the corner. People were starting to panic over their shopping and spending all day out and about. Eating at Hal's was quicker and easier than eating at home.

"You sure you got my shift on Christmas Eve?" Mary asked her in concern. "It's just that my mama always does a big thing and—"

"I got it," Melody assured her as she waited for her tickets to come up. "I wanted to work. I need the money."

"You've been working doubles every day," Mary said with a look of disbelief. "You can't be needing money *that* bad. I feel terrible 'bout Christmas Eve."

"Don't feel terrible. It's good. Works out better for me." Melody turned to look under the register for the spare box of straws. She grabbed a handful and stuffed them in her apron. "Besides I'd just be sitting in my living room all by my lonesome otherwise."

"You could spend it with Powerhouse over at the Conners. The three of them are a sad bunch on the holidays. Not a one of 'em seems to know what to do. None of 'em had a mama round growing up and it sure shows—Oh hey, Jules!"

"Hey."

Melody peeked past the register from her crouched position on the floor to see Jules leaning against the counter. Her long blonde hair was pulled back into a sensible ponytail today. She had a big pair of designer eyeglasses pushed up on her head. She wore an expensive-looking black business suit beneath her peacoat that was cut and tailored to her long, lithely muscular body. One eyebrow was arched at Mary, light eyes narrowed in an intense lawyer glare Melody found more than a little alarming. Between the two Conner siblings, Jules was definitely the more intimidating.

"I was sorta hoping you didn't hear all that," Mary said with a wince.

"If wishes were fishes," Jules said with a sad shake of her head. "Don't worry 'bout it. You got it spot-on; holidays ain't our thing."

"I thought you'd be at the fight," Mary said, a blush of embarrassment staining her cheeks. "You're always there."

"I'm heading out now. I just had a few cases to wrap up, stuff that couldn't wait." Jules leaned past the counter, looking down at Melody. "You got a minute?"

"Um," Melody started, knowing she was hiding from Jules, who wasn't just one of Clay's best friends but also had a pretty, pressed, extremely intelligent air that left her feeling uncomfortable.

"Melody, you're up."

Saved by the bell!

Melody jumped up and turned to the window as Hal put plates on the metallic deck. She grabbed them, doing a precarious balancing act, lining the hot plates up her arms. She ignored both the burn and Jules as she walked around the counter.

"It'll only take a minute," Jules called out. "I'll wait."

Melody got the message. Jules planned on standing there until Melody listened to what she had to say. She wasn't thrilled with that, but she was a little too busy to worry on it too much. She delivered the food to table four, then refilled the drinks at table six, and bused table five when they left. She was on her way to greeting new arrivals when Jules grabbed her arm, her grip firm, her small, manicured fingernails brushing against the bare skin on Melody's bicep.

"I gotta catch a plane," Jules told her, making it obvious she wasn't taking no for an answer. "And I just need a moment."

Melody heaved a sigh, looking to her tables and the new people waiting to be seated. Then she glanced at Mary, who was walking around the counter with plates in both hands. She gave the other waitress a look of consummate pleading. "Mary."

"I got it. Take a ten-minute break. This is probably as slow as it's gonna get," Mary said with a smile, turning to the family waiting. "Help yourselves to a booth by the windows. I'll be there to get your drink orders in just a sec."

Knowing this was her only chance, Melody followed Jules out of the dining room to a quiet corner in the hallway that led to the bathrooms. Melody leaned against the wall, the lull in work causing the exhaustion to slam into her. She blinked heavy-lidded eyes, trying to hide her desperation for sleep because she knew Jules would likely report back to Clay. She didn't want him worrying about her, especially when he had other things he needed to stay focused on.

It was amazing how heavy her body felt with fatigue. The stress of trying to save up enough money to leave Garnet before Justin found her took its toll. She was fighting a six-day-long tension headache and an ache in her back that came from constantly being edgy and on guard. Resisting the need to slide down the wall and quit fighting, Melody just waited quietly for Jules, who was digging in her purse.

Jules pulled out a small stack of papers and held them out. Melody took them, the words blurring under the weight of her tiredness. She saw her name and frowned. "What's this?"

"It's a ticket," Jules said simply. "It's a printed confirmation of your flight to Las Vegas. I had to upgrade to first class in order to get you a last-minute seat this close to Christmas."

"What?" Melody stared down at the papers in her hand, noticing not only the price, which was enough to make her faint, but the time and date the flight left. "This says the plane leaves in a few hours."

"Yeah, we gotta go." She gave Melody a pointed look. "Time is of the essence. I called Louise. She used to work for Hal, still does on occasion. She's gonna fill in for you while you're gone. Oh, there she is." Jules waved. "Hey, darling! Just go in back and tell Hal I'm paying you to work."

Melody felt like her brain was swimming. She leaned around the corner, looking to where Jules was waving, seeing an older woman walk in wearing a Hal's Diner uniform.

Melody glanced at the ticket once more, feeling guilty when she considered how much it had cost. "Look, I appreciate this, but I *need* this job."

Jules shrugged, looking collected and unruffled. "It'll be here when you get back."

Melody put a hand to her forehead, the tension headache pulsing stronger than ever. She was a little too overwhelmed with life to be dealing with Jules Conner. "I'm not good for him," she whispered, hoping to put the urgency in her voice. "Really, if you care about him, you won't push this."

"Do you care for him?" Jules countered. "Is his health and safety important to you?"

"Of course," Melody said a little too quickly. She wanted to retract it, knowing her passion wasn't helping her cause, but she couldn't help it. "Yes, of course, his health and happiness mean everything to me, that's why—"

"Then you'll come." Jules shrugged. "'Cause if you don't, he's gonna get the living shit beat out of him by a cocky city boy named Romeo Wellings. Have you ever watched an MMA fight? Do you understand how hardcore they are?"

"I'd never heard of it until Clay," Melody said with a wince, realizing how very little she knew about this sport Clay was so passionate about. "It's like boxing, ain't it?"

"Boxing's dangerous." Jules gave Melody a look that said she thought it was common knowledge. "So's MMA, and because of *you*, neither his head nor his heart are in this fight. If he goes into the octagon without your pretty self sitting there cheering for him, he's gonna get hurt, Melody; he's gonna get hurt real bad. Now are ya coming or not?"

Melody looked at the printed ticket in her hands and then thought of the big television Hal had set up in the dining room for the fight tonight. Why did she think she could run around and work while Clay was fighting with some city boy who saw Clay as the only thing standing between him and glory?

"I'm coming," Melody said breathlessly. She'd already stood by the wayside while one city boy beat the passion and joy out of her life, and she sure as hell wasn't going to let it happen again. She was mad at herself for even considering it. "Let's go."

"We'll run by your house and grab a few things. I got a spare bag in the car." Jules grabbed Melody's hand, dragging her across the restaurant and behind the counter. "Get your things. We gotta move like hell's breathing at our necks."

Melody didn't need to be told twice. She ran into the back to grab her jacket and purse. When she came back to the front counter, she handed her purse to Jules and then pulled her jacket on. "What 'bout my truck? I gotta follow you."

"Gimme your key. I'll get it back to your place," Hal said, coming out of the kitchen. "We got it, Mel, just go. Make sure our boy brings home another belt."

Melody felt dazed. Hal was standing there, Mary behind him, and the new waitress was also watching, having obviously filled them in on why she was there in the first place. Then Melody turned to look around at the restaurant, seeing all eyes on her. It was one of the most bizarre moments of her life.

"Keys," Jules snapped, dragging her back to reality as she held out Melody's purse, opening it for her. "Hurry, hurry."

Melody grabbed her keys and worked at undoing the key to the truck with shaking fingers. When she struggled with it, Jules huffed and grabbed the key chain, doing a far more effective job with removing it. "When's the last time you had some sleep? You look like you're about to drop where you stand."

"Been a while." Melody winced, knowing she must look a mess.

"You can sleep on the plane." Jules pulled the key free and tossed it on the counter. Then she shouldered Melody's purse and reached out, grabbing her hand. "We just gotta make it there first."

Melody was still dazed, the cheers rising up from the patrons sounding distant as Jules opened the front door, letting in a blast of cold air. She turned, seeing everyone standing up and clapping, the excitement palpable. It hit her then how important this fight was to this town, how important *Clay* was to them. He made Garnet interesting, and when he won, the whole town won with him.

It wasn't until she was out in the cold, the cheers from Hal's patrons a low hum, that she said, "Jeez, this town really does need a movie theater. I can't believe that many people know 'bout us."

Jules pushed a button on her key chain, making a shiny, silver Mercedes beep back at them. "You make sure Clay wins this fight, and he can *buy* them one. Get in."

Jules had a very demanding nature. It was easy to see why she was such a successful lawyer. Melody got into the Mercedes, feeling awkward when she was still in her waitress uniform. Jules jumped into the driver's side and was pulling out of Hal's parking lot before Melody got her seat belt on.

"He doesn't make that much, does he?" Melody asked, rather than focus on Jules driving, which was a little intense for her tastes. "Just for one fight?"

"One fight?" Jules gave Melody a bewildered look. "This is a title fight, and he's the UFC's top-earning fighter. You really have no clue, do ya? It ain't a lie. You really like Clay for Clay, bad attitude and all."

Melody prickled, feeling defensive as she glared at Jules. "I think his attitude's just fine, and if you don't know that, then maybe you ain't really his friend."

Jules eyebrows rose, shock showing on her face for one brief moment, before a smile tugged at her lips. "Darling, for Clay's sake, I sure hope things between you two work out, 'cause I think you might actually be one worth keeping."

Chapter Seven

"He doesn't know I'm here?"

Jules took a deep breath, looking up from the rapid texting she was doing on her phone. "He could get nervous. It'd be terrible for you to watch him get knocked out. Wyatt's holding it as his trump card. If Clay gets in trouble, he'll use it. But right now he's not certain if it'll throw his game. He'll play it if he needs to."

"But he wanted me to come," Melody reminded her, speaking loudly over the throb of people and music reverberating inside the dome. "He asked me himself."

"Did he invite you to watch the fight?"

Melody considered that, looking around at the massive crowd. She'd honestly had no idea Clay did something that attracted the enthusiasm and adoration of this many people. Clay's fight being the main fight of the evening thankfully bought them a little time. It was exciting, but it was also terrifying. She wasn't real sure coming to this fight had been a great plan. If she had to watch Clay get beaten and hurt in front of this many cheering people, she might get sick all over Jules's shoes.

"No," she finally said, feeling her heart in her throat. She wished she had better success with praying, because she'd never been more scared in her life than she was for Clay at that moment. "He said I didn't have to watch the fight. He thought I'd like Las Vegas."

"Yeah, I thought so." Jules sighed, sitting back against her seat, looking out to the octagon. "I'm gonna hear it later 'bout bringing you."

They fell into a tense, awkward silence after that. They were both uneasy. The pulse of adrenaline in the room was sky-high, and it was making Melody so nervous her knees were shaking. She pulled at the sleeve of the sweater she'd thrown on in the mad rush to gather her things before they left for the airport. It was a sure bet she'd forgotten 90 percent of what she really needed. As it was, a sweater for a sold-out arena in Las Vegas was a very bad decision. She was sweating like crazy. To ease the uncomfortable heat, she pulled out her hastily done ponytail and worked on tying it tighter and higher to keep her thick hair off her neck.

She was glad she did when the room burst to life. Lights flashing, announcer's voice echoing over the intercom, the music pumping with the bass beat of excitement. There was so much going on in so many different places it made Melody's mind reel.

"This is him." Jules pointed to the side of the arena where a group of men were making their way down a path that led to the cage in the center of the arena. "That's Wellings."

"They said his name's Romeo," Melody shouted over the throb of sound beating at her ears, the scream of the crowd deafening.

Jules pulled a face. "That's his first name."

Melody turned to watch the progression of the group. It was easy to spot the other fighter among his entourage. Walking at the center of the group, with obvious bodyguards flanking him on each side, he seemed handsome, sharp, and intense. Strangely enough, he reminded her a lot of Clay, with his cap pulled low over his eyes and his big, broad body. Only this fighter was more outspoken. He gave fans high fives and talked to the cameraman in front of him. There was a lot of male posturing, throwing out his chest, trying and succeeding in looking very intimidating. When he got to the ring and pulled off his cap, Melody had to admit he was very handsome.

Needing a distraction against the fear settled heavy in her chest, Melody leaned into Jules. "That's sorta an odd coincidence that his name's Romeo. Isn't Jules short for—"

"Don't say it." Jules turned to glare at her. "You know he's the enemy, right?"

"But...that was the coincidence," Melody started, finding herself looking into Jules's icy-eyed stare. "'Cause you're from different houses."

"No, I get it," Jules said sharply. "But if you believe in omens, you might wanna stop with the comparisons because Clay's from *my* house, and we want a different third act."

Melody frowned, trying to remember *Romeo and Juliet* from eleventh-grade English. She vaguely recalled Romeo killing a family member of Juliet's, and got Jules's point. The coincidence was a little too odd, and she decided to stop thinking about it before she gave herself heart palpitations.

"Well, I don't believe in omens," Melody said, needing it out in the air.

"Me neither," Jules assured her, though she sounded decidedly unsure. "Okay, here he comes."

Melody stood on her feet to watch as Clay and his team made their way to the center of the arena. The excitement was intoxicating. It seemed like the crowd screamed ten times as loud for Clay, and her heart was literally bursting with pride over it. It was amazing Clay had managed to achieve this level of success. She was awed this many people not only knew who he was, but were excited just to see him. All of Garnet treated him like a celebrity, but they were used to him too; many even avoided him because he gave off an intimidating air. Until this moment, Melody hadn't understood the sweeping scope of his fame, and it was surreal.

It felt like she had accidentally fallen into a relationship with a rock star.

Clay wasn't as dynamic as the other fighter. He didn't have the flash. He didn't posture to the camera. Wyatt, however, did. While Clay walked stoically to the ring, Wyatt jumped to give high fives to fans, looking enthused and pumped to be exactly where he was. Melody realized he was compensating for Clay's quiet intensity, and he was doing a damn good job of it.

Even with his cap pulled low over his eyes, Clay was easy to read. He seemed oddly calm and completely unaffected by the buzz of the crowd. His shoulders were stiff and straight. His stride was confident, and Melody hoped with all her being that he'd have a reason to remain so self-assured.

Clay and Romeo entered the ring.

She fell silent, feeling the pound of her heartbeat reverberating in her ear. Why had she agreed to come? Clay didn't even know she was here. A surge of cowardliness slammed into her, and she was desperate to flee before the fight started. The idea of Clay getting beaten by this man, of sitting there watching him take abuse she understood better than she wanted to—this was Melody's idea of hell.

"I can't do this," Melody said in a wild panic.

Jules just reached over and grabbed Melody's hand in a powerful show of unity, her grip shockingly tight. Jules squeezed her fingers nearly to the point of pain, making it obvious Melody wasn't the only one who wanted to run away.

"I've been to dozens and dozens of these fights, and it never gets easier," Jules said in anguish. "I'm so sick of this sport."

Melody had just been introduced to the sport, and she was already sick of it. She could hardly imagine poor Jules, who'd been watching both her brother and Clay compete for years and years. It was like witnessing a train wreck, seeing the two fighters facing off with only a referee to stop something truly terrible from happening. Melody was so frozen with fear the only thing she could focus on was Clay's bare chest, which was now slick and smooth. He must have shaved for the fight. His hair was shorter too, leaving it standing up in inky black spikes as he bounced up and down on his side of the ring, loosening his shoulders, his fists held up as the referee stood between the two fighters.

The referee in black stepped back, and Clay and Romeo met quickly in the center of the cage, their gloves touching. Then they both bounced out of reach, their stances springy, gloves held up. Melody could feel Clay's concentration from across the room, but Romeo's was also noticeably intense. It wasn't even surprising when he flew at Clay, looking like a wild bull, throwing his fist into Clay's jaw before he could respond to such a swift move.

Jules squeezed Melody's hand tighter. "Shit."

Clay punched back, but Romeo got two more hits. Romeo was stunningly fast for such a big man. He had a crazed air about him, reminding Melody of a street fighter, someone with nothing to lose. It was a boldness she didn't know if Clay could match. When Romeo threw another wild punch, Melody was about to close her eyes and pray for it all to be over, but Clay managed to push him against the cage before she could.

"Get him to the mat, get him to the mat," Jules chanted next to her as if silently willing Clay into action.

Romeo fought back. His knee continually kicked up, trying to jab at Clay's side, hitting suspiciously near his groin, but Clay held him there in a strange headlock, making her realize this was a very different sport than boxing.

"What is he doing?" Melody asked, wishing she understood more of what was going on.

"Take him down," Jules snapped in response, making it obvious she had eyes and ears for what was happening in the center of the arena and nothing else. "Get him to the mat."

Clay getting Romeo to the mat seemed really important to Jules, but it never happened. Romeo managed to maneuver away from Clay, fists flying in that wild fighting style that was terrifying because it was so fast and unpredictable. Melody might know very little about boxing and even less about Mixed Martial Arts, but she surmised one thing from watching the fight unfold. Romeo's power was in his speed and fearlessness, whereas Clay's was quiet, controlled, and structured. If Romeo was the hare, Clay was the turtle, taking hits, then pushing Romeo against the cage, obviously trying to wear him down. It just didn't seem to Melody like the turtle could win against this level of raw anger.

When the round ended, Melody found herself breathing a sigh of relief because it meant Clay was getting a reprieve from the pain.

"That round went to Wellings." Jules took a deep breath, obviously happy for a break from the tension of watching. "I dunno, Melody. This is, um..."

"Yeah," Melody agreed, understanding perfectly.

This was agonizing.

The break was brief. Clay sat in his corner, and a man Melody didn't know was doing something to a large, bleeding cut above his eye. Wyatt and Clay's coach Tony shouted a bunch of things, waving their arms around as they yelled, and Melody had to admit Clay looked pretty uninterested in whatever they were trying to get across to him.

She watched the close-ups of him on the big screen. Clay seemed more dark and brooding than ever. His chest glistened with sweat, his eyes hooded and intense as he stared ahead while his team yelled orders and the guy treating his eye did something to that cut above his eyebrow that *had* to be painful.

Clay might be getting his ass kicked, but he didn't seem to be too concerned about it.

If she were the opponent, that would be unnerving, especially to a man as wildly passionate as Romeo. When the second round started and the two men were facing off in the cage once more, Melody watched Romeo's face on the big screen. He was more traditionally handsome than Clay, with a smooth, Italian complexion and classic features. He watched Clay with trepidation as he bounced from one foot to the other, looking for the right moment to strike. There was a shiftiness to his presence that told Melody he might be more unnerved by Clay's stoic nature than he let on.

The second round went much the way of the first, with Romeo punching and kicking like a crazed beast whose very life breath depended upon it. Clay would retaliate by pushing him against the cage, holding him there until he broke away, only to hurt Clay once more. Clay's hits were minimal, his kicks even less so. He had another cut under his other eye to match the one above his eyebrow.

This was turning out to be, sadly, a one-sided fight.

Melody was starting to be glad she'd come to Las Vegas just so she could hold Clay after it was over, because this was horrible to watch. She wanted to look away, but she felt like she'd be betraying Clay if she did. If he was going to suffer through getting beaten in front of thousands of people in the arena and countless others across the country who were watching it on television, the least she could do was keep her eyes open.

Clay was back in his corner, his face still apathetic as they treated the new cut. Wyatt was yelling; then he was pointing to the crowd. It threw Melody off, her exhaustion working to her disadvantage. She was watching the interaction on the big screen instead of staring at them directly. She didn't figure out Wyatt was pointing to where she and Jules were sitting until Jules suddenly surged out of her seat, pulling Melody with her.

"She's here! She's here watching you get your big ass kicked!" Jules burst to life when she suddenly had twenty seconds to convince him Melody was really there in Las Vegas. She waved one arm, the other one holding Melody's hand in the air. "You see her! Tell me you see her!"

Melody's ears were throbbing. She'd had no idea Jules had lungs like that. Despite the pulse of light and sound, Melody was inclined to believe Clay really did hear Jules's screams. As it was, other people in the crowd were looking at them in stunned amazement, a murmur rushing through the crowd as Jules continued to jump up and down and demand attention in a way only a Conner could.

Like most people in the audience, Melody watched Clay on the big screen and saw him squint to see past the lights and the dark wire of the cage. Melody would have thought it was impossible to actually spy them in the crowd, even with Jules throwing the mother lode of all attention fits. She saw it with her own eyes, the recognition on Clay's face, the way his lips parted and the first emotion of the night passed over his features as his head whipped around and he glared at Wyatt.

"He saw us." Jules panted, a sob of relief bursting out of her. "It's gonna be okay. I think it's gonna be okay."

Melody wasn't so sure. She studied the look of sheer fury directed at Wyatt and was willing to believe Clay was going to beat someone, but she wasn't so sure it was Romeo Wellings.

Clay looked like he wanted to kill his best friend.

Jules sat, still breathing heavily, and Melody sat with her. She glanced around at the other spectators, seeing everyone staring at them. She felt like a bug under a very big microscope and turned back to look at the cage, watching the seconds tick by until the fight started once more.

Pretending to be invisible didn't work. The guy next to her, a big hulk of a man with a neck as thick as his head, leaned uncomfortably into Melody's personal space. He smelled strongly of beer. His gaze ran leeringly over Melody sitting there in her floral print dress and sweater. "You got a little crush on Powerhouse? You think you're his girl?"

"Back off, buddy," Jules growled, actually reaching around Melody to shove the man's shoulder. "Stay in your own goddamn seat."

"I'm a lot more available than him, you know." He ignored Jules's shove as he waggled eyebrows at Melody. "I'm a fighter too."

"Big fucking deal," Jules said menacingly, obviously not used to being dismissed. She leaned over Melody once more, light eyes narrowed furiously as she got in the man's face. "You look at her like that again, and I will *end* you!"

The guy pulled back, looking stunned at Jules's viciousness. Then he threw his hands up in a show of surrender. "Chill out, lady."

"You fucking chill out," Jules barked as she stood up and waved her arms to usher Melody to the other seat. "Move over. We're trading seats."

Melody wasn't going to argue with that. She took Jules's seat, glancing nervously around them once more, seeing they were attracting more attention than ever. She was starting to learn an outing with Jules was its own little adventure.

Jules fell down into her new seat, looking as pressed and polished as ever in her fitted black pants suit. She cast dark, menacing glares at her new neighbor, who looked genuinely scared of her.

"I think I wanna take some of those self-defense classes you teach," Melody said in awe, because that was one of the most impressive things she'd ever seen. If there was a class to give a woman that much self-assurance, she wanted to take it. "How much are they?"

Jules gave her a secret wink and smirk that was very reminiscent of Wyatt. "On the house."

With all the excitement, Melody missed the shuffle that brought the fighters back to the center of the cage. She looked up at the big screen, seeing Clay's scowl as he bounced up and down, waiting for the fighting to start. His eyes kept darting sideways, and it looked like he was looking to where they were sitting. Front row, they were pretty darn close to the cage. Melody had to wonder if he'd seen what happened with their neighbor, considering Jules's tendency to draw attention to herself.

Melody forgot the excitement with Jules when the fighting started. Much like the other two rounds, Romeo jumped at Clay, fists flying. Clay took the first punch and then threw his shoulder into the other guy, his foot hooking around Romeo's calf, knocking his feet out from under him. The sound of two heavyweights slamming to the mat made an echoing thud across the arena. It happened so fast Melody gasped out loud; one second they were boxing, the next Clay had Romeo flat on mat.

"Yes!" Jules jumped out of her seat, arms raised.

She wasn't the only one. The whole crowd surged forward at the first sharp jab of Clay's fist connecting with Romeo's jaw. Then Clay was beating on Romeo with intent, somehow holding the huge man pinned to the mat as his right fist flew hard and fast, hitting over and over again in a display of raw fighting skill that was remarkable. It was the first point in the fight where Melody covered her eyes, because it was too painful to watch. Clay was pounding on him like a jackhammer, beating at his skull faster and meaner than Romeo ever could. For his part, Romeo's arms flailed as if trying to deflect the rain of blows long enough to protect his head.

Then the energy in the crowd changed. A different sort of vitality surged through the arena that was tangible. The announcers were screaming, their voices bouncing off the walls, but the cloud of excitement made them hard to understand. Melody lowered her hands curiously, finding Romeo on the ground as officials hurried into the cage. Clay stood behind the referee, still looking harsh and intense, his chest rising and falling in hard, heavy breaths as if prepared to jump at his opponent once more.

"What happened?" Melody shouted over the roar of the crowd.

Jules turned to her, giving her a wide, bright smile. "He won!"

"Just like that?" Melody gaped. That was too fast after the past two rounds that had seemed to drag on for an eternity. "It's over?"

"It's over!" Jules confirmed, sounding breathless as she spoke loudly over the screaming crowd. "Hooray for jujitsu!"

Melody wasn't real sure what that meant, but she breathed a sigh of relief. She was glad to see Romeo get up, because she was half worried Clay had killed him. He even gave Clay a sportsmanlike half hug, telling her that at the end of the day, after all the fanfare and drama, this was still just a sport. Confetti fell from the ceiling, looking like living glitter under the strobes of colorful lights. Melody finally made sense of the announcer's enthused yells echoing over the crowd.

"*Clay Powers, reigning heavyweight champion of the world!*"

That seemed like a pretty impressive title for a man she'd fallen for over diner fare and coffee. Melody was a bit lost and awed as to how she got to this moment in her life. She felt dazed that she woke up this morning and headed to work, but somehow ended the night in Las Vegas watching Clay doing something most fighters could only dream about.

She thought the belt they put on him was gaudy and tacky and didn't match Clay at all, but she was happy he'd gotten it. The crowd never once stopped screaming. Even when Clay finally got out of the cage, the sound was booming. Melody's ears would probably ring for a week.

Then with cameras in his face and bodyguards flanking him, Clay walked over to where Melody and Jules sat facing the arena. Melody jumped forward and reached out to clasp his hands in hers. For one brief moment, time stopped. She and Clay were connecting as if she'd never tried to push him away to begin with, and it felt like her universe clicked back into place.

"Come on, come on!" Clay barked in his usual surly tone, pulling on her hands. "Hurry, Mel!"

Melody understood. There were people everywhere, pressing in against her and Jules. Everyone was trying to touch Clay. The second where time seemed to stop evaporated, pushing everything into fast-forward. Jules leaped over the wall and landed on her feet. Melody followed her, scrambling over the edge with far less grace, but Clay and one his bodyguards helped her down while other people screamed and reached out to Clay.

With two feet on the ground and the push of fans no longer crushing her, Melody breathed a sigh of relief. Clay leaned down, placing a chaste kiss against the top of her head, and she was grateful for it. She needed the connection, but there were too many people watching. Cameras and fans were everywhere. Melody would have died if he made a big production once he got to her.

But he was Clay, and he'd never do that.

Those damn cameras followed them all the way out of the arena and into the dressing rooms. They asked Clay questions that he gave clipped, one-word answers to. He was an amazing fighter but a horrible performer for the masses, and this sport seemed to require some level of showmanship.

Fortunately Clay had a snake charmer for a best friend.

Even after a championship fight, Wyatt didn't seem to have any problem drawing the focus away from Clay and making himself the center of attention. Tony worked on pulling off Clay's fingerless gloves and cutting the tape off his knuckles while Wyatt started running his mouth to the cameras.

"He was just biding his time. Biding his time and letting Wellings wear himself out," Wyatt was saying to the cameras, the twang to his accent stronger than ever, as if that was part of his act. "This ain't a street fight; this is a championship match. Clay took his hits and looked for a crack in the armor. When he saw it, he went for the takedown, and y'all saw how it ended. Wellings is a powerful fighter, but he ain't able to compete with someone like Clay, who's got a more balanced skill set. That boy's got no control, and his grappling's weak. All Clay had to do was get him to the mat."

"Was Clay playing it low-key on purpose?" one of the interviewers crowding into the little room asked. "Was that part of his strategy?"

"Wellings is cocky." Wyatt shrugged. "If he underestimated Clay, that was his poor strategy and it ain't got nothing to do with us. There's no trickery. Clay saw a weakness, and he capitalized on it."

"Hey," Clay said, coming up behind her.

Melody turned from watching Wyatt talk to the cameras. Having witnessed the fight without having a clue what was going on, she was genuinely interested in Wyatt's breakdown. But Clay clasped her hand in his, heedless of one camera still following his every move, and pulled her through the crowd.

"Come on."

He found the bathroom in the back of the room, ushered her in, then shut the door in the cameraman's face while Melody stood there gawking at him.

"They'll think we're being inappropriate," Melody whispered as Clay locked everyone out. "Is this allowed?"

"I don't really care." Clay sighed, turning away from the door to step into her personal space. His large hand slid to the back of her neck, his thumb caressing her jawline. His dark eyes studied her in concern. His scowl etched a deep impression on his forehead beneath the brim of his black cap. "Are you okay?"

"Are *you* okay?" she countered with a look of incredulousness. She reached up to delicately touch one of the cuts beneath his left eye. "Your face is sticky."

"It's Vaseline."

Melody frowned. "Why?"

"It keeps the skin from tearing."

Melody winced. "And, um, what's grappling?"

"It's ground fighting, like wrestling and jujitsu."

"And you're good at that?"

The first smirk of the evening tugged at Clay's lips. "Yeah, I'm pretty good at it."

Melody couldn't help but smile back, her cheeks hurting from the effort. She could hear the chaos outside, but all she knew was Clay's big body filled up the little bathroom and it felt so good to be surrounded by him again. She leaned into him, wrapped her arms around his bare back, and hugged Clay without a care for the sweat dripping off him.

She laid her cheek against his smooth chest and closed her eyes. "I don't like your chest all shaved."

"Me neither." Clay rested his chin against the top of her head. One hand caressed her long ponytail; the other rubbed her back soothingly. "And it itches like hell when it grows back."

Clay was sweaty and sticky and still humming with an obvious adrenaline rush. There was a whole room of people probably thinking they were doing something really inappropriate, to say nothing of the viewers across America watching the after-fight footage.

Melody was tired. She'd flown for the first time in her life today. She'd sat front row and watched a championship fight. She'd decided she was going to take self-defense classes if it killed her, because she wanted that raw self-confidence Jules had. It was a very eventful day filled with many things to think about, but all Melody could recognize was the low hum of happiness that filled up the bathroom because she was in Clay's arms again.

"Mel."

"Hmm?"

"Don't leave me again, okay?" Clay whispered in a voice choked with emotion as he pulled her tighter against him and tilted his head to rest his cheek on top of her head. "'Cause that 'bout killed me."

"I think Justin knows where I'm at. I'm pretty sure he's gonna come after me." She breathed a sigh of relief. Letting out the secret felt like breathing out the poison eating at her soul since she'd gotten the letter. "I don't wanna ruin your life too, but I'm so tired of being alone. 'S not fair, ya know?"

"So we'll deal with it together," Clay said simply, not sounding at all surprised by Melody's confession. "And if he comes after you, then I'll have finally found a good use for over twenty years of martial arts training. Good thing too, 'cause it was starting to feel like a massive waste of my time."

Melody squeezed her eyes shut tighter and laughed. There was a gaudy championship belt digging into her hip that said he'd already found a pretty good use for those skills, but the crazy thing was, Melody knew he meant what he said.

Chapter Eight

Melody had forgotten her toothbrush. The hotel gave her a new one. She'd packed all wrong for Las Vegas. Jules told her they'd go shopping while Clay and Wyatt played nice for the promoters. When she realized she'd forgotten a spare change of underwear, Clay suggested she go without, and she agreed that was a good plan.

She sat on the massive bed cross-legged, fiddling with the alarm clock, the cord stretched tight while she pushed buttons. She wore one of Clay's black UFC shirts covered in sponsors' logos, her legs looking pale against it. Her long hair hung thick and loose around her shoulders. It reminded Clay of corn silk. It had the same blonde, fluffy consistency. He loved it, because it was soft and welcoming, just like Melody. She pushed her glasses up on her nose and glanced at Clay, who made very slow work of brushing his teeth as he stood there in his boxer briefs staring at her.

"I can't get the darn thing to work," she said with a frown. "You think we can order a wake-up call every hour? Do they do that all night long?"

Clay pulled his toothbrush out of his mouth and said past the toothpaste, "I think for the amount of money this room costs, the hotel can send up an orchestra to sit outside the bedroom door and play Beethoven every hour."

"That ain't a lie," Melody agreed, falling over the bed to put the alarm clock back on the nightstand. Then she reached for the phone, studying the directory on the side before she put the receiver to her ear and dialed. "Hello, yes, I was wondering, do y'all do wake-up calls at night, 'cause we've gotta wake up every hour from now till morning."

Clay put his toothbrush back in his mouth, pretending to brush his teeth while staring at the way his shirt rode up as she lay on her stomach. Her milky thighs were exposed. He tilted his head, glimpsing the round curve of her ass.

"That's him. Didja get to see the fight tonight?" Melody asked, giving Clay a smile. "Yeah, he did good. Thank you, I'll tell him."

Clay rolled his eyes and went back into the bathroom to brush his teeth. If he stayed there watching Melody twirling her hair between her fingers and talking on the phone, he'd never get done. He made quick work of finishing up and grabbed a towel to better dry his hair. Melody was still on the phone with the front desk, which was sort of amazing. He tossed the towel down and fell into bed next to her. He lay on his side, propping his chin on his hand and giving her a pointed look while she chatted with the operator.

She must have gotten the point because she nodded in understanding. "Okay, well, I gotta go now. He's pretty tired, and if I'm being honest, I'm 'bout to drop too. It was nice talking to you." After saying good-bye, she clicked the receiver on the phone and turned to give him a smile. "The front desk guy is a big fan of yours. He knew all sorts of stuff 'bout you. He told me you used to be a wrestler in high school. Is that true?"

"Yeah, big deal." He gave her a bemused smile. "Lots of guys were wrestlers in high school."

"You were one of those popular jocks, weren't ya?"

"Not really," Clay said with a roll of his eyes. "Wyatt was the popular jock. He was handsome and outgoing and everyone loved him. I was the scary foster kid he hung out with."

Melody reached out, caressing Clay's still-wet hair, which felt nice because he had a massive headache courtesy of Romeo Wellings. He closed his eyes, feeling his heartbeat radiating out from the cuts the doctors had closed using thin pieces of clear medical tape. He knew he was looking rough, but Melody didn't seem to care.

"How come you were a foster kid?" she asked, still stroking his hair lovingly. "You never told me what happened."

"My mama had issues, and Garnet ain't exactly the best place to be an addict. The sheriff was always riding her. Big Fred was like Wyatt, a workaholic, nosy as hell, always up in everyone's business. She got tired of the hassle and took off without me."

"What'd you do?" Melody asked softly, her voice aching.

"She left me with her boyfriend of the month, thinking he'd look out for me, but he was a prick," Clay said bitterly. "So I ran away. Luckily it was summer. I slept outside, took showers at the Cellar. Course it was just the rec center back then. Used to steal food from

Mable's One-Stop Shop. I did all right considering I was only eleven. I lasted 'bout three weeks before it went to shit."

"What happened?"

"Wyatt happened." Clay let out a laugh. "I snuck into the rec center to use the facilities and take a shower. I didn't take any classes, but Wyatt practically lived there seeing as he had no mama and his daddy worked all the time. We ran into each other, which was unfortunate. The two of us weren't exactly friendly."

"Really?" Melody asked, her eyes wide in surprise. "That's hard to imagine."

"We were in the same grade, but we never got on. Jules was all right, but Wyatt was a cocky bastard I'd have hated even if his daddy hadn't been making my life hell for as long as I could remember." Clay rolled his eyes at the memory of a young Wyatt. "Believe it or not, he's mellowed with age. He used to have a real mouth, just unbelievable what'd leave it. So there I was, tired and hungry and dirty, and Wyatt's big mouth opens and says something 'bout my mama being trash. I punched him 'cause I was having a shit month and I was angry at life, but Wyatt'd been taking martial arts classes since he was old enough to walk. He kicked the living shit outta me. It was a really unfair fight, in front of half the kids from our class, no less. After that there ain't been any fight I could lose that'd be half as bad."

"Whatta jerk," Melody said with a scowl.

"Yeah, I'd be inclined to agree, 'cept Big Fred found out 'bout it and hauled Wyatt out to my house to apologize. Course, I wasn't there, and Big Fred spent all night looking for me. When he found me sleeping on a bench in the park, he took me back to his place. Turned out Wyatt was feeling pretty bad 'bout what happened. He told me flat out we were gonna be friends if I liked it or not, and I've spent the last twenty-two years trying to shake him."

Melody grinned, deep dimples appearing out of nowhere. "And you started taking classes with him at the rec center."

"Yup. Lotsa classes, mainly 'cause they let me beat on cocky ol' Wyatt Conner. Big Fred paid for 'em even when I was living with other folks. Maybe he thought someone oughta be taking Wyatt down a notch too. Then when the system was gonna move me to another town, Big Fred just went ahead and took me in 'cause Wyatt and Jules pitched the mother lode of all fits. I've been living there ever since."

"Then I'm happy he beat you up if it meant you got a family outta it," Melody said with a smile.

Clay considered that for a second before he reluctantly admitted, "Yeah, me too. But if you tell him I said so, I'll deny it. I'm still pissed off at him 'bout tonight."

Melody gave him a look of concern. "He was just worried 'bout you. You should forgive him."

"Nope." Clay rolled into Melody, who was still on her stomach. He rested his cheek against her shoulder, burying his face in her soft, sweetly scented hair. "You smell like cookies."

Melody laughed. "It's oatmeal honey shampoo."

His face throbbed, his head ached, and he was suddenly very tired. He tossed one leg over Melody and dragged his bare foot up the smooth line of her calf. He reached under the shirt she was wearing, feeling the slope of her ass, then moved up to caress the dip in her lower back.

"I'm falling asleep," he warned her, because unconsciousness was only a breath away. "I feel like I've been on a ten-day adrenaline rush that crashed and burned two minutes ago."

"Mmm." Melody hummed in agreement, making it obvious she was having the same problem as she pulled off her glasses and tossed them on the nightstand.

She stretched out beneath him. Her cheek rested on her folded hands. She seemed happy where she was, and Clay wasn't going to complain. His eyes closed to the drugging feeling of serenity being around Melody churned up.

And in what seemed like a few minutes, the phone rang.

Melody shifted, reaching for it and bringing the receiver to her ear. "'Lo? Um, yes, we appreciate it." She clicked the receiver back on the hook and then rolled over beneath him. "It's the wake-up call."

"Can't be." Clay groaned. "There ain't no way that was an hour."

"He said it was," Melody argued. "You wanna get under the sheets?"

Clay thought that was a brilliant plan. They shuffled to get under the sheets, shoving the comforter to the foot of the bed because it was a little too warm in the room for them. Melody set the phone back on the nightstand, and Clay rolled up to her, resting his cheek in the valley between her breasts.

"Move a second." Melody pushed at his forehead lightly. When Clay reluctantly lifted his head, she pulled the shirt off and tossed it to the floor. "Better?"

"Much." Clay's cheek now rested against smooth, bare skin, and he lay there simply feeling the warmth of Melody. He wrapped his arms around her waist and tossed one leg over hers, knowing she probably felt crushed. Right then Clay wished he'd been born a normal-sized welterweight instead of a big, hulking heavyweight. "Am I heavy?"

"You're fine." Melody stroked his hair, easing the throbbing at his temples and lulling him back to sleep. "Feels nice. Being with you is always nice."

Clay had to agree. This was quite possibly the nicest place he'd ever been in his entire life, and he wouldn't have been able to move even if he wanted to. He fell asleep as quickly as he woke up, thinking if that darn phone rang one more time, it was going to hit the wall.

* * * *

The phone rang—many times.

Clay didn't toss it against the wall, but only because Melody was the one closest to it. When the sky went from black to gray, Clay made it clear if the guy at the front desk woke him up one more time he was going down there in his underwear and use the clerk's head as a punching bag.

Melody told the front desk to stop with the wake-up calls.

But it seemed like she was apprehensive about falling back to sleep when the doctors had made it clear Clay had a concussion that needed to be monitored. With both of them more asleep than awake, Melody switched positions, draping herself over Clay. Her head rested against his chest; her fingers reached up to trace his face. They ran lightly over the taped cuts. Clay knew he probably looked worse as morning approached than he had the night before. He was happy it was mostly dark in the room.

Then Melody started kissing his chest, and he couldn't think to give a shit about anything but his cock hardening. He tangled his fingers in her thick hair and squinted to see past the near darkness of the room as she nipped one flat, dark nipple. Melody was naked and touching him, with her hand sliding down to trace the lines of his abdominal muscles, and it was *really* turning him on.

She lifted her gaze to him, her green eyes stark and vibrant in the near darkness. "Is this okay?"

Seeing her without glasses never stopped surprising him because she was so breathtakingly beautiful but somehow exposed in a way that appealed to him. He swallowed hard and nodded. "Yeah, it's um...great. I like when you touch me."

She gave him a smile, dimples peeking out beneath long blonde hair before she lowered her head and placed a kiss against the center of his chest. He pushed her hair away from her face, watching Melody place soft, tentative kisses over the muscles of his chest before she started moving lower.

Her tongue darted out, dragging slowly over the first ridges of his abdominal muscles, and Clay's breathing fell shallow. Lust and concussions didn't play well together. The throb in his head was more deafening than ever, but he wasn't going to tell Melody that. He was enthralled, his cock straining hard and swollen against the confining material of his underwear.

His stomach muscles clenched as she moved lower, licking and kissing her way to the elastic of his black briefs. His entire body was tense in anticipation. His gaze followed her every movement. His cock jerked at the way her pink tongue looked darting past full, lush lips. She was naked and bare and gorgeous, and it was taking more strength than he knew he had not to take control. He wanted to roll her over to taste and own her like she was doing to him, but he didn't. Clay lay there passively, letting her learn him, giving her the power to set the pace.

When she cupped him through his underwear, he nearly came off the bed. His eyes closed to the surge of desire, his head falling back against the pillow. She stroked him through the material, and he growled in response. His dick felt so fucking good in her hand, but the underwear was starting to seriously piss him off.

"Take 'em off," he said through clenched teeth, unable to curb his harsh nature when he was this turned on.

Melody tugged at the band, pulling it over his hips, sliding the briefs down, and exposing his cock. It slapped against his stomach, hard and eager, as Melody worked the underwear down his long legs. Once they were past his knees, he helped kick them off.

On her hands and knees, with long hair hiding full breasts and pink nipples, Melody looked more angelic than ever. Only now she was more reminiscent of a fallen angel, one who'd surrendered herself to a devil that wanted more from her than friendship and pie. Clay couldn't even feel bad for the corruption. He was completely captivated, and it felt okay. He saw the hunger reflected in her emerald gaze as she crawled back over him.

The lust and desire reverberated between them, making the need more intense with every raspy breath. Her eyes actually sparkled as they ran over his naked body spread out and exposed beneath her. Her smile was impish. Then she leaned down, grasping his thick cock, and licked the head. He groaned and thrust his hips into the caress of her hand, desperate for more. She took the invitation and sucked him, her mouth sliding down his cock in a slow, sensual stroke.

"Fuck!"

Clay jerked at the pleasure and reached up to fist a hand in her hair, holding on to her like a lifeline. He fought to keep his eyes open because that was the sexiest thing he'd ever seen—Melody's mouth on him, poised halfway down his dick before she slid back up and licked the head once more. When she sucked him again, this time taking him deeper, Clay lost his battle to watch. He bowed into the pleasure of her mouth, his eyes closing to the ecstasy as she started sucking and stroking him in earnest.

It'd been too long. His body began vibrating almost instantly. His balls were tight and pained with the need to come because Melody was *really* good at this. He wasn't expecting it. They hadn't been together long enough for him to have grown accustomed to the flare of passion. He felt blindsided by the pleasure and longing she churned up in him. He didn't think he could want this badly or ache this deeply until they'd fallen into each other's lives.

Teeth clenched, body tight, he fought once more to open his eyes. He watched her suck him, pink lips glistening as she took him in her mouth hard and deep over and over again. He let the memory etch itself into his brain because it was an exquisite sight. Then he used his hold on her hair to tug hard enough to force her to release.

"Come here." He groaned, knowing he was two seconds away from losing it.

Melody's breathing was shallow, her eyes wild as she looked up at him in confusion. "What?"

"Come here," he repeated and reached down to grasp her wrist. "Come here and lemme feel you, Mel. I need it."

Melody must have needed it too because she crawled over him without complaint. When she sat straddled over him, Clay leaned up to rest his weight on one open palm. He used his hold on her hair to tug her head back, and leaned down to feast on the thrust of her tits. He sucked on one pink nipple hungrily, his tongue laving the taut bud until it tightened against his lips.

"God." Melody bowed more deeply into the pull of her hair, offering herself up to him. "Why does it feel so good?"

Clay didn't have the answer to that, but he wasn't complaining about it, either. He moved over to the other breast, giving it the same harsh treatment, sucking and tugging lightly with his teeth until it beaded up. Melody was panting, shaking in his arms. She was so fucking responsive it drove him crazy.

He dragged his tongue slowly from her chest to the base of her throat and then used his hold on her hair to expose the gentle curve of her neck. He nipped and bit at the soft skin, her hair soft against his face, her moans making his cock ache for the first hard push inside her.

"Please, please, please." She writhed in his arms, her warm, wet pussy brushing against his dick, beckoning him. "Please, Clay!"

He brought her mouth to his. The kiss was hot, wild, uninhibited for the pulse of several long heartbeats before he pulled away and looked at Melody, needy and breathless over him.

"Go ahead." Clay's voice turned low and gravelly with sex. "Use it; fuck it. It belongs to you; own it."

Melody's gaze became molten, the pink sheen of morning painting itself over her flushed skin. She licked her lips, looking awed. "Is that true?"

"Yes," he assured her without hesitation. "I thought I was broken too, that I'd never trust women, but I had it all wrong. I wasn't broken at all. I was just waiting for you. It's always been yours; even before we met, it belonged to you."

Clay wasn't real sure if they were talking about his heart or cock, but it didn't seem to matter. Melody sucked in a sharp breath, her eyes glittering like emeralds as they filled with tears. She reached up, cupping his face in both her open palms. She kissed him, soft and sweet, as she shifted her hips, rising up higher on her knees until the head of his cock was pushing against the tight, warm opening of her pussy.

He tightened his fingers in her hair once more. He took dominance of the kiss, pushing his tongue into her mouth as an outlet. The pleasure of leisurely sliding into her wet heat, her pussy slowly stretching to accommodate his girth, was driving him insane. They were both shaking with the measured rise of bliss, feeding the flames on purpose, waiting until the pulse was too much to deny.

She clung to his shoulders, her small fingernails digging into the skin until he was buried as deep as he could go. Melody pulled back, looking between them, her chest still rising and falling with rapid pants of desire.

"I like looking at you in me," she whispered as if confessing a dark secret. "I dunno why I like it, but I do."

He leaned farther back on his open palm, giving her a better view of their bodies connecting. Melody sucked in a sharp breath in response, her gaze still glued to the place between them where his cock was buried deep inside her. Seeing her so enthralled with their joining was spellbinding. Clay couldn't have moved even if he wanted to. All he could do was look at her face, seeing her eyes grow glassy with passion and awed beauty over what she was witnessing.

With a low moan, Melody's head fell back, her hair tickling his thighs, making it obvious the sight became too much. Then Clay couldn't do anything *but* move. He thrust his hips up instinctively and clasped the round curve of her hip to pull her tighter against him. Melody moaned a second time as she fell back farther, her open palms resting against his legs, exposing the curve of her lush figure to his hungry gaze.

He slid his hand up her body and stopped to palm one round breast, brushing his thumb against her nipple. Melody used her grip on his legs to grind against him. Clay moved with her, offering his cock up for her enjoyment. He wanted to watch her get off on him, and he used Melody's pleasure as a distraction against his own rising hunger. He left her breasts neglected to trace his thumb around the swollen folds of her pussy. Melody shuddered, goose bumps spreading over her flushed skin.

He teased as she rode him, listening to her low moans, observing as her body tightened with the need to come. When he finally touched her clit, rubbing his thumb against it soft and fast, Melody cried out. Her body jerked from the powerful sensation. He expected that she'd give in to the rush of pleasure and fuck to a quick orgasm. Instead she adjusted to the intensity of the intimate touch and rode out the storm leisurely. Bowed back to the thrust of his cock, her movements remained languid as he teased her to climax.

Watching her with a heavy-lidded gaze, Clay continued to play with her body, spread out—beautiful and willing—in front of him. He rubbed her clit, stopping only to feel the slick stretch of his cock buried deeply inside her as she ground against him. Melody's breathing became sharper, more desperate. Her skin grew dewy with a fine sheen of sweat.

The rise was so slow the pinnacle was a surprise.

When Clay went back to concentrating on rubbing the tight bud hiding between her folds, Melody suddenly cried out, her body shaking, her pussy pulsing around him. Wave after wave seemed to roll over her, drawing out low, sweet sounds of surrender that nearly pulled him down with her. Instead he rode out the storm, thumbing her clit until she fell over the edge, then caressing the smooth lines of her naked body when the rush simmered down to slow, quivering pulses of bliss.

When he felt the last of the tension fall out of Melody, he sat up, wrapped both arms around her back, and pulled her to him. She was languorous, obviously needing the extra support. She twined her arms around him, burying her face in the curve of his neck as she tried to get her breath back.

If he wasn't so fucking desperate, he would have let her cling to him all morning, but seeing her let go like that, watching the ecstasy build and build, he was half out of his mind with lust. Still holding her to him tightly, he reversed their positions.

Clay pushed her against the mattress before reaching down and then grabbing her thigh. He spread her wide as he pulled out and thrust into her in a hard, carnal mating he couldn't tame. Melody screamed in response, her back arching, her fingers tangling in his hair. He started driving into her, hungry for his own taste of oblivion after the forced separation between them.

His body strained; the pump of his heartbeat reverberated through him stronger than ever. He was blind to everything save the need to fuck Melody, a helpless slave to his own pleasure. He would have been angry about the weakness if Melody wasn't right there with him, driven and yearning, her hips moving with every slap of skin against skin.

Melody's moans became sharp, hard gasps of pleasure, and he knew she was close. He fucked her harder, his grip bruising as he pumped his body into hers. She tensed, her nails dragging across his back, her body shuddering with a second orgasm.

Clay was lost.

He fell into the chasm, the pleasure pounding, the throb of it making white spots form in his vision. He fisted the sheets as his cock pulsed, filling Melody with the warm, sticky evidence of his pleasure. He shuddered and moaned in her arms, surrendering completely to the cataclysm of ecstasy.

It destroyed him.

It left him bare, exposed, and humble in the face of it.

He loved this woman.

There was no other explanation. It wasn't even surprising. It felt like something he should have known all along. All he could do after the revelation was collapse over her, utterly spent. His words were gone, stolen with his breath. He knew he was heavy and eventually gathered enough good sense to roll off her. He fell onto the bed next to Melody, a hand splayed over his chest, still rising and falling in sharp, hard breaths that lingered after the crash.

His head felt like someone had taken a sledgehammer to it.

Clay knew there was probably something to be said, some profound words of undying love and devotion that were protocol when you found the other half to your soul. Instead he rolled into her because not touching her was agony. His cheek rested between the valley of her breasts once more. Her heart was still beating faster than usual, and he listened to the thump of it, feeling his eyes grow heavy.

"That was nice," Melody finally whispered into the glow of early morning filtering in past the open windows.

"Yeah," he agreed, already half asleep to hide from the headache. "Thank you."

Melody stroked his hair in response, lulling him to sleep as effortlessly as she'd pulled him to passion. She gave so willing of herself. Everything she had to offer was his for the taking, and it didn't feel like a robbery. Everything he had to give was hers too. Clay could lie here, and he didn't have to say anything.

She already knew.

Chapter Nine

After the early morning sex, the rest of Clay's slumber felt more like a power nap than anything, but he wasn't complaining. He had a hard time sleeping too deeply once the sun rose anyway. He was naturally a morning person.

When the phone rang, Clay reached over to answer it himself, seeing that Melody was still asleep.

"Yeah?" he whispered into the receiver.

"Hey, Clay, buddy. How you feeling?"

Clay pulled a face. Even after sex and winning a championship belt, his agent's voice grated on his nerves. "What'd ya want, Rick?"

"I just wanted to make sure you were up and moving."

Clay groaned. The promotion bullshit. He'd forgotten about it in the wake of getting back together with Melody. He wanted to be with her all day, not playing nice for sponsors and fans.

"Clay?"

"I'm up," Clay said rather than complaining, because he had a contract that said bitching about the obligations was pointless. "How much time have I got?"

"Couple hours."

Clay hung up the phone and then glanced at Melody, who blinked tiredly at him. She brushed her hair out of her face and then gave him a lazy smile. "You didn't say good-bye to your friend."

"He's not my friend; he's my agent."

"Does that mean you don't gotta be polite and say good-bye before hanging up?"

"That's exactly what it means," Clay said with a smirk. "He makes an obnoxious amount of money off my blood and sweat and knows better than to complain 'bout my bad attitude."

Melody gave a laugh of incredulousness. "That ain't nice."

"More often than not, I ain't that nice." Clay winced, hoping it wasn't too much of a shock to hear it. "You wanna try out that big ol' tub in the other bathroom?"

Melody grinned, looking perfectly fine with his confession of a long history of rudeness. "I'd *love* to try out that tub with you."

Clay was struck by how nice it was to wake up with Melody. Playing domestic with her was something he could get very used to. He wanted every day to start by watching her crawl out of bed naked and padding barefoot across the room. He admired the way she looked from behind—with her long hair hanging thick and loose down her back and the gentle curve of her ass taunting him out of bed.

Melody stopped at the bedroom door, turning around to arch an eyebrow at him. "Are you coming?"

"Yeah." Clay rolled out of bed and stretched. He grinned when he spied Melody squinting at him. "You want your glasses to get a better look?"

She surprised him by smiling and nodding. "Hand 'em to me."

He picked her glasses off the nightstand and walked them over to her. Melody put them on, looking adorable wearing the black frames and nothing else. Her gaze ran over him boldly, making Clay's cock stir. Forget the championship belt; spending most of his life keeping himself in peak physical condition felt more than worth it just to get Melody to look at him like that, with stark appreciation showing in her lustful gaze.

"You are one fine-looking man, Clay Powers," Melody finally announced, giving him a mischievous grin. "Even all bruised and battered, you're mighty nice on the eyes."

Clay looked down at himself, seeing a large bruise over his rib cage, but not much else. Most of the damage was to his face, which was still throbbing this morning. He winced. "I probably look rough."

"It ain't that terrible." Melody shrugged. "I wish I'd have remembered to bring you some vanilla extract. It's my mama's remedy for bruises, and you wouldn't believe how well it works."

Clay gave her a look. "I heard a lotta remedies for bruises, but I ain't never heard of that."

She laughed. "I know, sounds weird, but it does work. I used to bathe in the stuff so much I spent four years walking round smelling like a sweets bakery. I tested it for ya—many times."

He felt his heart drop when he realized *why* Melody used to douse herself in a home remedy for bruises. There was a man out there who'd hit this beautiful woman enough times that she flinched when someone grabbed her arm or came at her too fast.

How inhuman did this Justin have to be that he could willingly hurt someone as open, sweet, and genuinely kind as Melody? Clay bruised people for a living, and he couldn't possibly fathom how anyone could raise a fist and hurt *her*. It literally boggled his mind, but it was suddenly very real to him in a way it hadn't been before, and he stood there physically aching over her past. He wished he had a way to erase it, but he didn't.

"What's wrong?" Melody frowned, making it obvious she sensed the change in him. "Do you have a headache? I know headaches like that get worse when you stand up."

He nodded mutely, not wanting to do anything that damaged the blanket of coziness that had fallen over them since the fight. He knew it was a gift that Melody felt comfortable enough around him to openly talk about the darker sides of her past, and he wanted to keep it like that. He'd be damned if he gave her a reason to censor herself just because he couldn't stand the thought of her suffering.

"You want one of those pills the doctor gave ya?"

Clay shook his head, still fighting the horrible realization that someone used to hurt Melody. Maybe it was really falling in love with her that brought it home. Maybe it was needing her like air or admiring her for being everything he wasn't. Whatever it was, he had to swallow past the lump in his throat before he could speak. "I don't like those pills."

"But the doctor—"

Still fighting with the rush of emotion, Clay blurted out, "My mama used to crush up pills like that and inject 'em into her veins at the coffee table. I don't like 'em."

"Oh." Melody gaped for one long moment before she recovered and turned to look into the main area of the suite. "I think I saw something else on the counter out there."

"I know I got ibuprofen somewhere."

"Then I'll get that for you," Melody said with a soft smile. "You wanna start the bath?"

"That's a good plan," Clay agreed, still feeling dazed.

Clay did as told and headed to the other bathroom to start the bath. He stood there holding his hand under the big, curved gold faucet as he tried to pull himself together. He wanted to shake it all off and pretend nothing bad had ever happened to Melody, but couldn't. When Melody came into the bathroom, holding out a bottle of water triumphantly, he had to force a smile.

"Ibuprofen." She opened her hand and showed off two white pills. "To cure what ails ya."

He took the pills from her. "Thank you."

"It was easy enough." Melody crawled into the big tub without preamble, looking excited. "Would you believe I ain't never been in a Jacuzzi? I certainly never took a bath in one."

Clay swallowed the pills. Then his smile turned genuine as he watched Melody sink into the tub with a low groan of pleasure. Her hair floated in the steaming water, looking like spun silk dancing around her.

"Dang, this thing is deep. I hope I don't drown." Melody gave him a teasing smirk as she took off her glasses and set them on the edge of the tub. "I don't swim."

"I swim," Clay said warmly, staring down at her as she stretched out in the tub. He admired her beautiful body beneath the ripples of water and battled once again with the rush of unaccustomed emotion. He hadn't thought it was possible to care for someone as deeply as he did for Melody, and the vulnerability terrified him. He'd do anything to protect her. "I won't let ya drown."

"Where'd you learn how to swim?" she asked as Clay climbed into the tub.

Melody scooted forward, letting him settle in behind her. Then she leaned back against his chest and put her feet up on the rim of the tub. She heaved a contented sigh and turned her head on his chest. It was obvious she was still sleepy and not as inclined to wake up early like he was.

"Ain't you ever looked around the Cellar?" Clay asked curiously. "It's got an indoor pool."

"Yeah?" she asked in a heavy voice. "I never noticed it. That's odd."

"It used to be a rec center. We got swimming lessons all year long and a Jacuzzi."

"That's a pretty fancy place to own." Melody reached behind her, grabbing one of his hands and pulling it around her until it was resting over the soft plane of her stomach. "How'd you buy it?"

"They were gonna close it down, and that place was a haven for us when were growing up. We couldn't just let it rot to the ground. Wyatt, Jules, and me went in together and bought it. It was looking rough by then and cost more to remodel than to buy it. We renamed it because it was a brand-new place when we were done."

"Dang, you three must be loaded if you're fixing up big rec centers with pools and Jacuzzis."

"We do all right," Clay confirmed. "But the Cellar doesn't make us much. We were happy when it started to break even every month. Now we make a little profit, but it's really a labor of love."

"I think that's nice. I'm sure Garnet appreciates you for it." Melody sighed, sounding more asleep than awake.

Clay let her lie against him in silence. The tub was huge, but with both of them taking up space, it filled up fast. He had to shake Melody when it reached the point that the water needed to be turned off. The way she jerked from his gentle nudge made it obvious she'd fallen asleep. She stretched out her legs, struggling to turn off the faucet with her feet in a way that was comical enough to make Clay laugh out loud.

Melody finally gave up, laughing with him as she leaned forward and turned off the faucet by hand.

She fell back against him with a huff. "Darn faucet. I ain't never seen a tub I couldn't turn off with my feet."

"Is this a specialized skill you've developed?" Clay asked, the mirth still heavy in his voice because he'd never once attempted to manipulate a faucet with his feet.

"Yes, it is," Melody said with another laugh. "I love baths, and I've become an expert at taking them. I used to have a big garden tub in Ohio, and it was the only highlight of being married to Justin. That tub was my escape. It didn't have jets, though. How'd ya turn them on?"

Clay turned around, searching for a button to turn on the jets rather than focus on the sinking feeling in his chest that blossomed once more. He found the button and pushed it, making the big bathtub burst to life.

Melody actually squealed in excitement as she placed her feet over the jets at the front of the tub. "If I was sad 'bout not having a tub at my little place back home, I'm real broken over it now. I could get used to this."

Hot tubs reminded Clay of sports medicine, and he wasn't overly thrilled with them. Being in one usually meant he was hurting pretty damn badly, but he was excited for Melody. She seemed to be genuinely enjoying the experience, and he had to admit lying in the bubbling hot water with her snuggled naked against him could easily change his mind about them.

He tried to focus on those things, the good things, rather than the tightness in his chest, but it wasn't working. Clay couldn't seem to stop himself from dragging it out in the open, because he didn't want any walls up between them.

"Mel." He finally sighed in defeat. "Will you tell me 'bout Justin?"

Melody turned around, looking surprised rather than affronted. "What'd you wanna know?"

Clay shrugged, feeling shy. "I dunno, just anything—everything. Does that make me an asshole?"

Melody considered him, her green eyes, so stark when they weren't hidden behind her glasses, seeming distant. "No, you're not an asshole. It's just not, you know…a nice story."

He wrapped both arms back around her and held tight because he knew her past was haunted and he felt guilty for asking. When he was uncomfortable, he tended to get silent. This time he found himself actually wishing for Wyatt's gift of gab because he couldn't think of anything to say to make things better as Melody turned around and settled against his chest once more.

"My daddy got sick," Melody finally whispered over the hum of the jets. "And it was terrible 'cause he was so big and so strong and he took care of us. I wish you could've met him, Clay, 'cause he was a real good man. He never said much, but his heart was golden. He'd give someone the shirt off his back if they needed it."

Clay smiled. "Sorta like someone else I know."

"Justin was smarter than me. He knew all the right papers to fill out. He helped get my daddy taken care of and made sure he didn't waste away in some run-down home. Justin helped make his last days as good as they could be. I appreciated him for it, but that was a dumb reason to marry a man I knew I didn't love."

"You never loved him?" Clay asked, his voice catching because saying it was harder than he anticipated. "Not once?"

"I liked him, but I never felt that spark like I feel with y—" Melody paused, her body tensing for one moment before she sighed. "No, it never felt right, but everyone kept telling me it *was* right. My mama loved him to death. She still does. She thought he'd give me all the things my daddy never could. She's one of those who always wants more than what she's got, and she thinks all that matters in life is how much stuff you have. I guess I heard her tell me enough times that he was the right one and eventually I started believing it. I wasn't old enough to listen to my gut. I learned that lesson."

"I learned a few of those myself," Clay had to reluctantly agree. "I think we all do."

"It wasn't that bad at first. It was never a fairy tale, but it wasn't terrible. Then we moved away and he changed. It just sorta started to build up once we got to Ohio, and I never noticed how really bad it was until it was too late." Melody reached down and squeezed his hand in the water as if searching for strength. "It started off with yelling after a bad day at work, insulting me, calling me fat, lazy—"

"You're not fat." Clay tensed in insult. "And no one can call you lazy."

"Someone can," Melody said with a bitter laugh. "Someone *did*."

"You're gorgeous, Mel," he reiterated because hearing Justin had the gall to call her fat had Clay wanting to pulverize him. Vulnerable or not, he couldn't help but admit, "Sometimes I look at you and think my heart's just gonna burst with how beautiful you are."

Melody turned around, giving him a surprised smile. Clay reached out to push a wet strand of hair off her cheek and tucked it behind her ear. The pause had Melody taking a long, shuddering breath. She fell back against his chest and started talking again as if his simple compliment gave her the strength to finish.

"He started hitting me, but he'd say sorry later. I believed him 'cause I really didn't think he wanted to hurt me. I thought it was work and stress and money because he's like my mama—always wanting more." Melody shook her head, sounding raw at the memory. "I made all sorts of excuses, and eventually I just got used to it. The hitting. The insults. The forced sex. I'm not proud of it, Clay. I hate that I let myself be a victim. I wish I was like Jules—"

"Jules ain't perfect," Clay reminded her. "None of us are."

"I felt trapped. I had no of money of my own. No car. No friends. He controlled everything, and my mama never believed me when I told her how cruel he could be. When I finally started hinting at the physical stuff, she called up Jason at work and he convinced her I had some sort of mental imbalance. She still believes that. I haven't talked to her in over a year."

"If she's thinking that, then not talking to her ain't really a loss," Clay said bitterly, feeling a hatred for Melody's mama bloom inside his chest to rest next to the hatred he carried for his own mother. "She gave birth to you, and she should've believed you."

"He's very charming. Smarter, savvier people than my mama's been fooled by Justin, but I know I can't trust her. She'd tell him where I'm at faster than you could blink."

"How'd you get away?" Clay asked.

"I said something at a doctor's office and ended up in a safe house for abused women. It was a miracle," she said, her voice lightening. "I didn't know there were people out there just waiting to help me out. You wouldn't believe how nice the ladies at the shelter were. They restored my faith in humanity 'cause most of 'em were just volunteering. They didn't get paid. They were there out of the kindness of their heart, and I sure wasn't gonna waste their effort by going back to Justin. Lots of women do, you know? They go back, but not me. Once I was out, I never looked back."

Clay hugged her tight once more, understanding what a huge achievement that was, to face the unknown because she knew she deserved better.

"I didn't have anything. Just the clothes on my back and what few things I'd carried around in my purse. I left everything behind. My grandmother's ring, the necklace my daddy gave me on my sixteenth birthday—I lost all of it."

"Don't ever wish to be anyone but you. You're amazing." Clay's heart hurt for Melody and everything she'd gone through, but he was unbelievably proud of her too. "You had the courage to know you deserved something better, and you followed through with it. That takes guts."

"Does it?" Melody asked, her voice suspiciously tight.

"I think so," he whispered, his voice as strained as Melody's.

Clay's eyes stung. He found himself fighting a strange battle of emotions, pride warring with pain, love for Melody pitting itself against a rabid hatred for her ex-husband. The past was the past; it was over. Clay knew he probably should have let the memories lie, but he was happy he knew what had happened in Melody's life that had led to their paths crossing for the first time on Thanksgiving.

"Clay?"

He took another long breath, still struggling to pull himself together. "Yeah?"

"Make love to me."

He didn't even need to think about it. He knew Melody was right. That was what they both needed. He turned off the jets and stood, making Melody gape as she looked up at him. Then he leaned down to grasp her arms and pulled her to her feet.

"What 'bout the tub?" Melody asked and then gasped out loud when Clay suddenly swept her off her feet. Her arms flew around his neck. Her fingers dug into his skin as she squirmed in his grasp, turning her head to look down. "Are you sure you ain't gonna drop me?"

"I'm sure," Clay said as he stepped out of the tub.

Melody clutched at him tighter, seeming stunned he could do something as simple as step out of the tub while holding her. "Clay, you're wet and that tile's slick and—"

"I gotcha," he said with confidence. "You're safe, Mel. I promise."

Clay felt the tension fall out of Melody. She slid one hand from around his neck, down the slick rise of his chest. She placed her open palm over his heart as she whispered, "I am now."

Clay had to take another deep breath to fight the sting in his eyes, and he walked across the suite with her as a distraction. He laid her down on the bed, then stood there staring at Melody with a sheen of goose bumps dancing over her pale skin and wet hair clinging to her full breasts.

He got that sensation again. His chest expanded with the emotions, making him feel like he'd shatter right there over how beautiful she was and how desperately he adored her. It actually choked him with the force of it. If he tried to speak, he'd lose it.

Instead he crawled onto the bed with her, savoring the feel of her wet, bare skin against his. He flattened his palms against the bed on either side of her head, and he studied her once more, seeing she was fighting the same level of emotional rawness. Her green eyes swam like sparkling emeralds, making it obvious she was near tears.

He leaned down and kissed her before it could get farther than that. Melody kissed him back with the same passionate enthusiasm she always had when they were together. Only now Clay understood just how amazing she was for embracing the passion between them when sex had been unkind to her in the past. She trusted him. More so, Melody trusted *herself* enough to know everything about this was right even if most people thought it was all wrong, and he wanted to make sure that trust was well-placed.

Right then he wasn't a fighter and she wasn't an abuse survivor. They were Clay and Melody, and their histories evaporated for the moment. He broke the kiss to move down her body. He pushed wet hair aside to lave his tongue over the taut, rosy peak of one breast. He sucked until it puckered against his lips, and Melody made a choked sound of pleasure.

Her fingers threaded into his hair as he moved over to the other breast, sucking and teasing once more. Melody shifted impatiently, making low, throaty sounds of desperation, and Clay understood she needed something more than slow seduction. He felt the same rabid need for mindlessness.

Clay released the tightened peak and grasped her waist in both hands. He lifted his head to look at her. "Tell me what you want, Mel."

Melody's chest heaved. Her hair was a tangle of honey blonde that clung to her face and shoulders. Her eyes were glazed with hunger. "Can you, um—" She licked her lips as her cheeks flushed with embarrassment. She leaned up on one elbow and then reached out, running a finger boldly over Clay's bottom lip. When he parted to her and licked the pad of her finger in the same teasing way he'd licked her clit, Melody sucked in a sharp gasp of desire and whispered, "Lick me."

He nipped her finger once more before a smile forced its way past the lust and emotion. Knowing she enjoyed his mouth made his cock swell harder than it already was. He moved down her body to slide off the bed and fell to his knees on the floor. He wanted to taste and lick her until she was writhing beneath him. He suddenly needed to feel her come against his lips like he needed air to survive. He knew his tongue couldn't lave away all the pains of the past, but he was already starved for her and desperate to try.

He used his grip on her waist to pull her closer. Melody spread her legs enthusiastically and exposed herself to his hungry gaze. Clay groaned as he looked at her, open wide and waiting for him. He almost couldn't breathe against the rush of lust. He was tempted to reach down and fist his dick against the urge to come because the sight in front of him was enough to push him over the edge.

"Clay." Melody reached down and ran her fingers through his hair, pushing it off his face. "Is this okay?"

"God, yes," he said quickly, knowing his stunned silence could be misunderstood. "You're just really—"

Beautiful. Gorgeous. Wonderful. Amazing. Perfect—Clay fought for the one word to sum up the wild rush of sensation surging through his bloodstream.

A smile quirked at Melody's lips. "Really what?"

Clay took a shuddering breath and let his gaze run up from her perfect, pink pussy to the smooth lines of her naked body, her lush hips and full breasts. Finally his eyes met hers. "Really sexy. You're sexy, Mel. So fucking sexy you blow my mind. I feel like I'm gonna come just looking at you."

Her smile blossomed and dimples appeared, making her entire face luminous. She was so open and trusting, so loving and radiant. Clay was awed by her and completely enthralled. He felt drawn to her pleasure like a moth to flame, and he couldn't resist the lure to lean down and suck on her clit.

Melody gasped and arched into the caress of his mouth. Her legs spread wider. Her fingers fisted in his hair, holding him to her. He never gave her a chance to catch her breath and adjust to the pleasure. Instead he ran his fingers over the folds of her pussy, opening her to the assault as he licked and sucked and drowned himself in the sounds of Melody's bliss.

Clay was so turned on his cock literally hurt, but he ignored it. He wanted Melody to climax hard and fast and violent as if the battering of ecstasy could wash out the bad memories he'd forced her to drag up. Small, broken sobs of pleasure burst out of her, mingling with half-formed phrases of pleading and appreciation. He felt the tightness in her body, the strain for release, and finally broke through the resistance by pushing two thick fingers deep inside her. Melody tensed, her head falling back against the mattress, her entire body curving upward from the ferocity of her climax.

"Clay!" she screamed, her hold on his hair tightening to the point of pain.

Melody's entire body shook. Her pussy fluttered and clenched to the pulse of her climax, and Clay thought it was a minor miracle he didn't come from the sight and sound of it. When he sensed her pleasure had crested, he pulled Melody even farther down the bed until her ass was at the very edge of it, and then sprang to his feet. He grabbed her legs, opening her wide.

He was mindless, wild, and hungry for the first drugging thrust that connected him to Melody. Being one with her was his ambrosia, his only addiction, his unique salvation. He didn't even have a chance to prepare her before he was giving in to the weakness and plunging his cock deep into the tight, slick heat of her pussy.

Melody bowed to his thrust, a shocked gasp of ecstasy tearing out of her.

Clay's head fell back under the tidal swell of pleasure. Then he was moving, letting Melody's gasps and moans fuel his own raging need as he fucked her hard and fast, erasing everything except the blinding pleasure.

Melody's body enveloped him over and over again as he slammed his hips against hers. His chest heaved. Sweat mingled with the lingering aftereffects of the bath. He could've come at any moment. The push of it was right there, threatening with every raspy breath, but he resisted until the moment when Melody abruptly shuddered with another orgasm.

He squinted against the need, seeing Melody's head thrown back as she fisted the sheets and shook even more violently with the second surrender.

Clay fell easily.

He moved his hips to the throb of pleasure as he spilled inside her, surrendering completely to the hum of release. He never stopped being amazed at just how good it felt to come while buried deep inside her, and it didn't matter that he was torn open and drained once more. If a climax with Melody was a small death, it was a death worth dying, and Clay rode it out until the end. He relished the pulse of pleasure, savoring every tiny aftershock of bliss until he felt like he'd bleed his soul into Melody.

The pleasure was cleansing once it ebbed to a warm buzz of contentment. He finally pulled out of her to crawl onto the bed and insure he wasn't the only one who felt renewed. He was relieved to see Melody looked as satisfied as he felt. The flush of pleasure still stained her cheeks. Her eyes were closed, her face serene. Clay reached out and pushed wet wisps of hair off her forehead as he studied her. She blinked, revealing sated green orbs that stared up at him with a gratified happiness he wanted to remember forever.

"Better?" he asked.

"Yeah." She touched his lips once more and smiled. "Thank you."

"No, thank you," he said with a laugh. "You heal me, Mel."

Her smile grew broader. "Ditto."

Chapter Ten

On the first day of the rest of her life—Las Vegas was the place to be.

Melody found herself awed with the lights and sounds. It pulsed with a life that was energizing. The casinos smelled like cigarette smoke, stale perfume, and adrenaline. It should have been off-putting, but oddly enough it compelled her.

The thrill drew Melody in, and she watched the gambling like a voyeur. Being on the outside let her see the excitement of the risk was in the not knowing, in the wild wish that this roll of dice would be the one that solved life's problems. After it was over, win or lose, wasn't nearly as exhilarating as those few heartbeats before the cards were dealt.

Hope was perfect. It was untouchable. Untarnished.

If only life would always exist in the space between the risk and the outcome. She wanted to stay in Las Vegas forever. It was the space between for her and Clay. The lever was pulled; the slots were spinning; there was no going back. They were suspended in the place where hope flourished. The past didn't seem to matter, and the future could be magnificent.

Or she could lose everything.

But the pulse of Las Vegas didn't recognize fear or failure. Its very air reeked of possibility. The impossible seemed effortless in Sin City. Insurmountable problems had simple solutions, and she fell for it as easily as all the other naive dreamers who showed up on the strip hoping for a better tomorrow.

"You could gamble if you want."

She turned to Clay as he leaned on a pillar at the edge of the casino next to her. Melody smiled, finding him handsome even if the aftereffects of the fight showed on his face. It wasn't the first time she'd seen him cut and bruised. Melody was starting to think the evidence of battle was part of his mystique.

"That's okay. I just like to watch."

She turned back to the casino once more, watching two old ladies sit side by side at slot machines. One had a cigarette in her mouth; the other held a cup of coffee. Melody was pretty sure she'd seen both of them in the casino before she left this morning doing the exact same thing.

"Do you wanna play?" he asked, studying her curiously. "I'll give you money to play. I'll even play with you."

"Do you gamble?" Her eyebrows rose in surprise. "I know you come here a lot."

"Not usually, no." He looked out to the casino with disinterest. "If ya wanted to, I would. It could be fun."

"Well, I don't think I'd like betting my own money." Melody laced her arm through Clay's and leaned into him. "But I like seeing 'em win. It'd be exciting to see someone win really big, like a million dollars or something. I'd love to watch that happen. That'd change their life."

"You'd think. But it doesn't. Money's just money. It don't change much 'bout who you are."

"Shoot." Melody laughed. "You're just saying that 'cause you ain't broke."

Clay reached out, fingering a lock of her hair she wore down just because she could. He tugged on it playfully. "You ain't broke neither; you know that, right?"

"Not today," she agreed, her smile still bright because the slots of her life were still spinning. "Today's perfect."

Clay laughed and tilted his head away from the casino. "You ready to eat? They're probably already sitting down."

Melody winced. "Why didn't you say something? I don't want them to wait just for me."

"You were having fun." Clay pulled his arm free of hers only to drape it over her shoulders. "Jules said you've been peeking in at casinos all day."

"Not all day," Melody argued as they turned and walked away from the casino. "I bought this dress."

Clay smirked as he eyed the new ensemble. "It's sexy."

Melody's new dress was black with white polka dots that flared out from the waist, hanging loose and flowing down to her calves. She'd got heels to match, ones with black straps that wrapped up around her ankles. Her hair was too thick to wear down without something to push it back, so she'd bought a glittery headband to keep the thick locks off her face. Melody felt very pressed and fancy this evening. Three hundred dollars was more than she'd ever wanted to spend on an outfit, but Jules, armed with Clay's credit card, insisted Melody needed to look good, and she was inclined to agree.

Melody looked behind them, making sure no one was listening before she told him teasingly, "I bought new underwear too."

"Too bad."

"Oh, they're racy, though," Melody said proudly. "I shocked myself."

"Yeah?" Clay's eyebrows rose, and he tilted his head as if trying to look down her dress. "How racy?"

Melody covered her shoulders with the sparkling black shawl she'd bought to combat the slight chill in the air. She laughed at Clay, who was now bending back, as if the outline of her ass in her new dress would give him a hint of what was beneath.

She looked around once more. It was starting to become a twitchy habit here. It seemed everywhere they went in Las Vegas, someone knew who Clay was. Even if the admirers didn't walk up and say something, they still hid in corners gawking and whispering. Sure enough she spotted two young men pointing in their direction. They nudged each other, looking hesitant.

"You wanna blow off dinner with the dynamic duo and order room service instead?"

"What?" Melody glanced away from the young men to look up at Clay in surprise. "But aren't they waiting for us?"

"So what?" Clay asked with a scowl. "I'm still mad at both of 'em. Let 'em eat alone."

"You should forgive them," Melody said firmly, feeling new warmth in her heart for both Wyatt and Jules now that she knew they'd been there for Clay when no one else was. "They're your family, and you gotta forgive family. I forgive my mama for siding with Justin."

"Yeah, well, I don't forgive my mama," Clay said cynically. "And I sure as shit don't forgive *yours*. You're a better person than me 'cause I got half a mind to call her when we get back to Garnet and let her know what I think of her."

Melody put a hand to her forehead, wondering if she should have let her secrets out to Clay, who took it all very personally. She was still humming from the aftermath of their last time together this morning before life reared its ugly head and forced them apart. Clay and Wyatt had dealt with promotional responsibilities while Melody spent the day with Jules shopping and exploring the wonder that was Las Vegas. Dinner was the first time she and Clay had really spent together all day, and she sure didn't want to waste it talking about her mother.

"Calling my mama wouldn't fix anything."

"Probably not," he agreed. "I wouldn't do it, but I like to think 'bout it. I like to think 'bout nailing Justin to a beam in the Cellar and beating on him till he pops too."

Melody pulled a face. "Ouch, Clay, that's gruesome."

"Sometimes I'm gruesome." Clay shrugged unapologetically. "Sometimes I'm a real mean son of a bitch, and he might wanna take note of that if he plans on coming to Garnet and harassing you."

"Powerhouse."

Melody frowned, turning with Clay's arm still heavy over her shoulder to see the two young men she'd spotted by the casino. They'd obviously followed them. Despite the boldness, they looked nervous as they fidgeted and met each other's eyes as if proud of themselves for actually approaching Clay.

"That's you, right?" the shorter of the two asked, looking at Clay critically. His gaze stopped on the taped-up wound on Clay's cheek. "You're Clay Powers."

"Yup, last I checked." Clay nodded. "Can I help you?"

"Well, um..." Their eyes met, the short one shifting from one foot to the other. "We were sorta wondering—"

"They want an autograph," Melody finished because Clay seemed impatient, and the boys were looking jumpy. She pulled away from Clay to open her purse. "I stole a pen and pad from the hotel. Hold on."

"Thanks," said the taller, gangly one, who was barely twenty-one if not younger. He gave Clay a broad, excited smile. "We were at the fight last night.

It was sick the way you took down the Gladiator in the third round like that. *Best fight ever.*"

"The Gladiator?" Melody asked, still searching in her purse that really needed to be cleaned out.

"Wellings," Clay supplied.

"Oh, right, 'cause he's Italian. I get it." Melody passed the pad to Clay and then looked in a side pocket, finding the pen. She handed it to Clay triumphantly. "I was starting to think my purse had eaten it."

"I can't believe you brought a pad and pen with you," Clay said as he pulled the cap off the pen.

Melody grinned. "I knew you'd run into someone who'd need it."

"Right." Clay turned to the young men, giving them a painful look that seemed to be his attempt at a publicity smile. "And what're y'all's names?"

The men gave him their names; they asked questions; Clay shook their hands. Melody found it all very exciting. Clay seemed so huge next to the other men, larger than life, with his black UFC hat pulled low over his eyes. He stood almost a head above both of them. His arms were massive, stretching the sleeves of his T-shirt; his chest was broad and powerful. She took for granted just how tall and fit he was. Garnet bred them broad and tall. At home he wasn't quite so unique, but here he stood out.

When the men got all their questions answered and Clay complained about dinner reservations, they parted ways. Melody waved to them as they left. "Bye, it was nice meeting y'all."

They waved back. The short one named Charlie called out, "Nice meeting you too!"

Melody turned back to Clay once they were out of earshot. "They were nice."

"You think everyone's nice," Clay said with a laugh.

"That's the reason I let you buy me this dress," Melody announced as they came up on the restaurant. "I didn't want you to look bad having some dumpy waitress on your arm with all these fans everywhere."

Clay turned around, giving her a horrified look. "You're not dumpy."

"I see all those women wanting your attention," Melody told him, feeling her cheeks heat. "I saw 'em last night. I saw 'em at that promotional thing y'all did this morning before Jules and I went shopping, and I see them all over this hotel. Watching you, waiting for the right moment to get you alone."

"I don't like those women. I like you," Clay told her, his eyes studying Melody with trepidation. "I never met anyone like you, Mel. First time I saw you I thought you were an angel, and I'm still not all that sure you're not."

"That's sweet." Melody smiled. "I think you're sorta blind, 'cause some of those girls are pretty eye-catching, but still sweet."

Clay shook his head, still looking horrified. "I would never—"

She reached up, squeezing his big hand in hers. "I know."

Melody's smile grew broader because she did know. She trusted Clay completely, which most people would think was naive, but she didn't care what others thought. No one could understand the companionship they shared, and she sort of liked it that way.

Clay took a deep breath, his gaze still running over her face before he nodded, obviously believing her trust in him. "Okay."

"Are you gonna buy me dinner or not?" she asked him teasingly. "I'm starving."

"Absolutely," Clay said, giving her a genuine grin rather than the pained grimace moonlighting as a smile he reserved for fans. "I'd love to buy you dinner."

He didn't know how hard it was for her to surrender and let him pay for things. Instinct would have her fighting tooth and nail against any man controlling her financially, but it was just dinner and a dress and he wasn't Justin. Both her heart and her soul knew that even if her mind was screaming to beware. This was Clay, and like he said, everything was okay…at least in Vegas.

* * * *

Dinner was at one of those fancy steak houses most people wore suits and ties to. Unless you were the UFC heavyweight champion of the world. Then apparently a black T-shirt, worn-out jeans, and sneakers were acceptable.

Melody had never been so glad for the new dress. If for no other reason than she and Jules being done up balanced out their dinner companions. Clay and Wyatt didn't appear to realize or care that by dressing down, they attracted even more attention than they would in suits. The dinner jackets the restaurant had loaned them and insisted they wear were now tossed over the backs of their chairs. Both of them seemed perfectly content to eat their eighty-dollar steaks and have everyone pointing and staring at them as they did so.

"Where'd Tony and Jasper go?" Melody asked curiously, thinking of Clay's coaches, who'd been with Clay for all his promotional obligations. "They've been hanging on you all day. I thought they'd join us for dinner."

Wyatt laughed. "They say they're gambling, but I think the betting odds are against that. They're blowing off steam somewhere."

"Ah," Melody said with a grin. "I suppose this is the place to do it."

"True." Clay lifted his head to give her a conspiratorial look. "They're doing something highly inappropriate; I'm sure of it."

Melody laughed and looked to Jules, who was eyeing her steak with blasé disinterest. Jules took another bite, chewing it thoughtfully as she glanced around the restaurant, obviously aware of the whispering and pointing that was coming from the other patrons. Not that she seemed too concerned with it or the inappropriate deeds of Clay's coaches.

"You know," Jules started as she reached for her glass of wine, "for the amount of money they expect for this meal, I ain't all that impressed."

"What's wrong with it?" Wyatt asked, pulling a face at Jules's plate. "Looks fine to me."

"Maybe it's just me." Jules took another long drink of the burgundy liquid glittering under the dim lighting. "But if I pay eighty bucks for a piece of meat, that thing better vibrate. I want long-lasting satisfaction outta the investment."

Melody coughed into her glass of wine and had to cup her hand to her mouth to stop herself from laughing out loud. She knew Wyatt and Jules had started drinking while they'd waited, but she hadn't realized how much it loosened Jules's tongue until right then.

"Thank you, Jules," Wyatt growled, pulling a disgusted face as he tossed down his knife and fork with a loud clatter that likely drew more attention. "You've just ruined a perfectly fine meal and totally grossed me out in the process."

"Bonus," Jules said, looking pleased with herself as she took another drink. She turned to Melody conspiratorially. "Like they can get high-and-mighty 'bout that. I do their laundry half the time, and neither one of 'em can throw stones over what I got hidden in my happy drawer. Some of those towels were looking pretty—"

"You might wanna dig into that steak," Clay said, looking up from his plate to give Jules a pointed look. "'Cause you're drunk."

"Nah." Jules shook her head. "I'm just buzzed."

"The second you start talking 'bout your happy drawer with Wyatt and me in the room, you're drunk. That should be your red flag," Clay said with a sad shake of his head. "Pretty soon you're gonna start talking 'bout your past boyfriends, and we're gonna have to excuse ourselves."

Jules considered that for one long moment before she sighed. "It has been a while. I'm 'bout to call one of 'em up, even if they were all worthless. Half of something's better than all of nothing, you know?"

"No, I don't know," Melody said, trying to follow Jules's reasoning and be polite.

"Small." Jules leaned into Melody, holding her thumb and forefinger an inch apart. "I'm cursed. 'Cept this one guy in college, but I was drunk—"

"Sorta like now," Wyatt intercepted, eyes wide.

"And he wasn't that good." Jules sighed. "Big dick, untalented tongue, bad, bad moves. Isn't thrusting a natural male instinct? How hard is it to get right?"

Melody looked behind her, because Jules's voice carried. She couldn't tell if they were pointing because of Clay and Wyatt or Jules and her unlucky bout with men. Either way she couldn't fight the amused laugh bursting out of her.

Clay looked nonplussed by Jules's dramatics as he turned to Melody. "Makes ya wish she'd stuck with the happy drawer."

Jules huffed, cutting at her meat with lackluster interest. "Chances are I'm gonna die sad, old, and alone. There ain't no guy in Garnet who wants me as his girl. I'm gonna spend the rest of my days living with my *brother*."

They all fell silent after that. Melody's heart hurt at the confession. She realized how intimidating Jules could be. Most folks in Garnet liked her and everyone depended on her, but she didn't appear to have any real friends. She was the only lawyer for two towns. Jules could handle anything from divorce to setting up a business, and it seemed to Melody that she did it really well. Jules was just too married to her work.

Wyatt stared at the table unseeing, as if considering Jules's ominous prediction. He reached out and picked up his wine. He downed half the contents and then reached for the bottle on the table to refill his glass. "I think you may have put me off steak for life. Thanks for that."

"Aw, don't fret, Wy. Hal could always hire another pretty waitress. Look at Clay. We didn't think he was ever getting himself a real girl, but lo and behold. Then again you'd done gave away your heart a long time ago, didn't ya? There ain't any pretty waitresses in your future." Jules let out a bitter laugh, giving Wyatt a wide, crystal-eyed stare of pity. "You're dying old and alone with me."

"Yeah, that's real funny." Wyatt glared. For the first time since Melody met him, he seemed subdued and dispirited from his usual sparkling personality. "Laugh it up. It's gonna be a real riot when you're crying 'bout your pathetic love life to the porcelain god in your hotel room."

"Oh, you're getting nasty," Jules said with a wince, not looking too put out by the hostility. "Touched a sensitive spot, I think."

Wyatt took another long drink of wine, all his usual good humor gone as he narrowed light eyes at his sister. "Fuck you, Jules."

"Aren't ya glad we decided to have dinner here instead of order room service?" Clay asked Melody with a false civility. "And I was pissed off at them *before* the server let them drink."

"I won you that fight," Wyatt said defensively. "You'd have lost if it weren't for Jules dragging Melody here. You needed motivation, and I provided it."

"That's just it; it matters more to you," Clay said sadly. "Maybe you do gotta try and move on. Work and fighting's all you got. You can't pine for Tab—"

"You've gone soft." Wyatt cut him off. "It was a fucking miracle Wellings didn't kill you."

"Whatever." Clay shrugged, looking back to his dinner, his jaw clenched for one long moment. Then he lifted his head, glaring at both siblings across the table. "Neither of you won me that fight. *I* won 'cause I spent most my life working hard at it, and Melody ain't just some pretty waitress. She's a lot more than that, and just 'cause she ain't got a fancy sheriff's badge or a bunch of diplomas hanging on her wall doesn't mean you can talk 'bout her like that. She's got grit and she's got courage, so until either of you know what it's like to leave *everything* behind 'cause you know you deserve better, you need to just shut your traps."

"I didn't," Jules said quickly, looking abashed. "I mean, she *is* very pretty, but I know she's more than that. I didn't mean—"

"It sure sounded like you meant it." Clay growled, giving both of them a furious glare. "You're embarrassing me seeing as how you two's the only folks I got to introduce her to as friends *or* family. You need to stop drinking and eat your steak."

"It's okay, Clay," Melody whispered, seeing the pity party for what it was.

Wyatt and Jules were both lonely individuals, and until recently Clay had been right there along with them. They felt like they were losing one of their own, and it was magnifying their isolation from a world that took a lot from them and gave very little in return. She reached over, clasped Jules's hand in hers, and squeezed tightly.

Jules squeezed her hand back, giving Melody a watery smile. "I like you a lot, you know that, right? I'm so happy Clay found someone to love him."

"I like you too." Melody smiled back at Jules indulgently. "But don't be telling people I love him; I ain't even told *him* yet."

She turned and looked to Clay hesitantly, wondering if her words were too bold. Clay met her gaze head-on. The relief in his dark eyes was palatable. The smile tugging at his lips was genuine and pleased. The tension fell out of his shoulders, and he broke eye contact to look back down to his meal. He picked up his fork, stabbing at a cut piece of meat, and Melody got the message loud and clear—he loved her too.

Chapter Eleven

Melody was starting to wish she'd gone to the Clay Powers's school of social graces. There was a wicked side of her that wanted to know what it was like to slam a door in people's faces, with a clipped *Time to fuck off*.

Clay leaned a hand against the door of the suite, looking skyward. "Conners shouldn't drink. Christ, whatta train wreck."

Melody laughed, covering her mouth with her hand as she pressed her ear to the door. She could hear Jules and Wyatt arguing down the hallway as they walked to their rooms, because both of them had voices that could wake the dead.

"Do you really think they're gonna die alone?" Melody asked when she was certain they were too far away to hear her through the door.

"Maybe." Clay shrugged, seeming to consider it for a moment. He winced, a look of genuine sadness crossing his gruff features. "Probably."

Melody sighed because she liked both of them. Even Wyatt's smooth-talking ways weren't so bad. At least he attempted to use his charisma for good, which was more than she had to say for most charmers. And

Jules was bold and outspoken in a way Melody admired. The idea that neither one of them had another half out there was suddenly very depressing.

Feeling guilty for laughing a second ago, she left the foyer and walked to the main area of the suite. One wall was nothing but massive panels of glass, leaving the entire room open to the skyline at night. While Melody would never want to live in the city again, even one that was as enlivening as Las Vegas, she'd always had a thing for city lights at night. She couldn't imagine anywhere with more color and lights at night than Las Vegas. She sat on the bench facing the floor-to-ceiling windows and took in the magnificent scene.

Clay sat next to her. He pulled his cap off, tossing it on the bench. Then he reached out, grasping her hand and holding it in his. "You never know what time will bring. Wyatt and Jules could find someone, maybe when they least expect it. I thought I was gonna die old and alone too, you know?"

Melody took a shuddering breath and turned to look at him. "Me too."

He squeezed her hand tightly in his, giving her a secret smile. "Not if I have anything to say 'bout it."

"How'd this happen?" Melody asked in a stunned whisper. She never expected to fall in love and certainly not this swiftly or with this much finality. "We just met."

"I don't believe that," Clay argued as he turned her palm over in his and traced the lines of it with the pad of his finger. "I'm pretty sure we've known each other forever. Seeing you the first time was like coming home, and there ain't been anything to happen since that's disabused me of the notion."

"Yeah," Melody agreed, the bright skyline blurring to a sea of vibrant color. She remembered seeing Clay in Hal's Diner the first time. Alone and eating his turkey, she'd been compelled to reach out to him. "Do you really believe in soul mates?"

"I do now."

Clay leaned into her, his fingers threading into her hair at the nape of her neck. Melody was pliant, letting him pull her to him. When he captured her lips, she parted to the thrust of his tongue, already lost to the white-hot current of attraction that constantly pulsed between them.

Clay tasted like dessert and expensive red wine. Melody was drunk with him the moment they connected. She'd waited all day to get to a place where she was one pulse, one throb of desire with Clay. She hiked up her dress and straddled his hips without reservation. Melody threaded her fingers into his short black hair and took control of the kiss. She pushed her tongue into Clay's mouth, and he groaned at the domination. It was a wildly empowering moment, having such a tall, strongly built, truly dangerous man quivering and yearning for her.

She gripped his shoulders, part of her mind measuring the wide breadth of them. Her center literally throbbed from the knowledge that he was hers. It was the first time they'd been together where Melody wasn't half-dazed with exhaustion. Clarity brought the realization of just how beautiful Clay was. He was the perfect specimen of male power and strength. Every inch of him hard and commanding, his form was a massive work of art. Melody felt sexual and feminine having him hot and hungry beneath her.

She broke the kiss long enough to tug on the back of his shirt. She wanted all those beautiful muscles on display. She wanted to see them under the lights of Las Vegas. With Clay's help, they pulled his shirt over his head and tossed it to the marble floor.

Bare-chested, he leaned forward, cupping Melody's face in his large palms, and kissed her again. He was just as hungry, just as needy for closer contact. Melody let him own her mouth, savoring him. It was easy to give herself to Clay when being with him made her feel nothing but cherished. It was even sweeter because she knew she owned him too. They belonged to each other, and the realization made the moment all the more poignant.

Clay yanked at her shawl, fighting with the knot, until finally she broke the kiss to tug it over her head and toss it to the floor. The struggle with the shawl loosened her headband, and she pulled that off too, throwing it on top of her shawl. Her glasses ended up on the bench next to Clay's hat, because she couldn't afford to step on them later.

Clay groaned as he brushed her hair away from her face. His palms were warm and calloused against her cheeks. His dark eyes studied her, and Melody really wished she wasn't half-blind without her glasses.

"You're so beautiful, Mel," Clay whispered, his low voice almost aching with emotion. "I love you."

Melody sucked in a sharp breath. Icy-hot pleasure spiraled through her bloodstream. Her chest actually hurt with the feelings welling up inside her, making her feel like she might shatter in his arms. It was too much; the emotions overran every thought, leaving her shaking from the onslaught. This was crazy. Things like this didn't happen—not to her. It felt too good to be true. She didn't want to trust it, but she couldn't seem to help herself.

She leaned into him and buried her face in the curve of his neck to inhale his scent. It gave her strength to finally say, "I love you too—more than anything."

Clay gasped. Melody felt him quivering also. It was a surreal moment, almost dreamlike with the bright glow of Las Vegas glittering around them in the dark room. Neither of them could find anything to say more powerful than what they'd already confessed. When Clay pulled at the zipper on the back of her dress, she heaved a sigh of relief. She couldn't say more than she already had, but her body throbbed with the demand for an outlet from the rise of emotions choking both of them.

The price of the dress forgotten, she struggled to be free from it. She slid off Clay, her high heels clicking against the marble as she pushed the dress down her body, then kicked it aside to lay with the rest of his discarded clothing.

"Christ."

Melody looked up at Clay's low growl. He studied her standing in front of him in nothing but a black, lacy bra and panties and her high heels. She could actually feel his look of raw hunger; it vibrated off him so strongly it made Melody breathless. Goose bumps danced over her skin. Her pussy throbbed.

Clay stood, and Melody gasped, her eyes closing to the frenzied rush of lust. One large hand wrapped around her waist, and the other threaded into the thick hair at the nape of her neck. Breathing heavy, Clay pulled her to him.

The first hot press of his mouth against the base of her throat made Melody actually cry out. "God, Clay!"

He bent low, licking at the curve of her breast, his tongue running along the edge of her bra. Her tits overflowed the black, lacy cups, and Clay feasted on the offering, biting and nipping, but it wasn't anything more than a tease when Melody was so pent up. She reached behind her and unlatched the bra, then pushed Clay away long enough to pull it off. It hadn't hit the floor before Clay was cupping both breasts, his thumbs brushing over her nipples, making them bead with pleasure. Melody moaned, desperate to be touched.

Clay buried his face against her neck once more, his lips pressing warm kisses to her fevered skin. "I wanna make you feel good."

"You're doing a pretty darn good job of it." Melody panted, feeling the cold glass against her back. She arched against it, pushing her tits deeper into Clay's hold. "I feel like I'm gonna—"

Her words ended with a choked gasp when Clay fell to his knees in front of her. Melody stared down at him in stunned disbelief as he took one taut nipple into his mouth. She was starting to wonder if a woman could come just from visual stimulation. The sight of Clay on his knees, bare-chested, sucking her tits with a look of fervent hunger on his face was one of the sexiest things she'd ever seen. When his teeth scraped against her nipple, she was forced to give in to the rush. She let her eyes close as she tossed her head back against the window, robbing her of the erotic sight.

Melody tangled her fingers in Clay's hair, holding him to her as he sucked and teased. Every nerve ending in her body jumped alive, as if Clay was somehow the antidote to a lifetime of mundane at best and heartbreaking pain at worst. She felt vibrant and alive as his lips moved lower, his hands tracing the line of her rib cage. When his hand slid beneath the line of her panties, Melody's cheeks flamed because she was embarrassingly wet.

Clay groaned at the first slick feel of her. His forehead pressed between the valley of her breasts as he breached her pussy, two thick fingers sliding deep inside, stretching her. "Fuck, Mel."

"I'm sorry," she whispered, biting her lip against the ecstasy of being finger fucked by him. "I just—"

"Don't be sorry. Never be sorry." His breath was warm against the curve of her breast. "You wanna get off on my fingers?"

Melody nodded breathlessly. "Yeah."

His fingers curved up, pressing against a place inside her that made her gasp at the stun of pleasure, and Clay capitalized on the discovery. His large palm spread over the curve of her lower back and forced her into the thrust of his fingers as he put pressure against that one sensitive place over and over again.

She gasped, her entire body shaking as she clung to him just to stay on her feet. "I can't take it. It's too intense, Clay. I can't—" She cried out once more, bowing to the pleasure of him finger fucking her. "Oh God!"

She couldn't fight him anymore. He wasn't listening anyway. The build of pleasure was a strange sort of burn, one that boiled and raged at her center, then pulsed outward until her entire being was consumed. She was wound so tightly Melody heard herself shamelessly begging as she started rutting her hips against his hand. She knew he could feel her pussy quivering with the need to come, and she didn't care. All she could think about was finding release from the rising tide of ecstasy.

Clay started sucking on her tits again, his teeth scraping and tugging at her nipples, magnifying the pleasure to the point that she had no choice but to give in. When the climax slammed into her, Melody screamed from the velocity of it. Clay tightened his hold, obviously sensing how completely weak she was to the ecstasy surging through her bloodstream as she quivered and shook in his arms. Stars actually danced behind her closed eyelids, and what felt like a lifetime of stress drained out of her tense body to the rolling tide of bliss washing over her.

When the wave started to ebb, Melody slid down the cool glass until she was on her knees in front of Clay. She didn't even get a chance to catch her breath. Clay fisted his hand in her hair, dragging her mouth to his and kissing her. He thrust his tongue into her mouth, and she opened to it, the connection making her blood stir with a fresh swell of yearning. His desperation was rousing, palpable in the very air around them as he pulled away, his broad chest heaving. Then he avoided looking at her, turning his head away to stare to the floor.

Melody knew he was fighting with himself, trying to rein in the rage of hunger that always erupted between them. It could be overwhelming. Melody knew because it scared her too, but she didn't want him to fight it. She craved all of Clay. She needed to see every dark part to his soul. If he'd fallen over the edge of control, she wanted to feel the chaos with him.

She reached out and ran her fingers over the hard lines of his abdomen. Clay tensed when she undid the button to his jeans.

"It's okay." She pulled his zipper down, revealing the hard, thick length of his cock straining against the band of his underwear. "I love you. I love everything about you."

Clay turned back to her, his features tortured with need. She saw the surrender as he cupped her face once more. She tasted the need when he leaned in, harsh and demanding as he kissed her. She slipped her hand past the band of his underwear, stroking the impressive size of him, and heard the ultimate defeat of his iron control in the low, pained moan against her lips.

He pulled at her panties, pushing them past her hips and down her thighs. "Get 'em off. I want both of us naked."

Melody was inclined to agree. She liked being naked with Clay. There was freedom in being bare and vulnerable beside him. She lifted her legs and struggled to get the panties off, catching them on one heel before finally tossing them aside. When Clay jumped to his feet and pushed at his jeans, Melody brought one leg up.

"Don't." Clay's eyes narrowed at Melody's hand on the buckle to her shoe. "I like 'em."

Melody looked down at the high heels, with their black straps wrapping around her ankles and up to her calves. A smile tugged at her lips. "Well, okay then."

"They're sexy." Clay pushed his jeans past his hips, taking his underwear with them. He toed off one sneaker, kicking it aside as his gaze ran over her. With one knee still raised, Melody was exposed to him, and Clay stared with unabashed intensity. "*You're* sexy."

Melody's smile grew broader as she looked into his eyes. She slid her fingers between her legs, touching herself and spreading the folds of her pussy wide open to his greedy gaze. Clay sucked in a sharp breath in response, stopping work on his shoes and jeans to watch. Feeling deviant and sensual in a way that appealed to her, Melody slid one finger inside. She did it for his benefit but ended up arching into her hand, her eyes closing from the sensation when she was still so sensitive from her first climax.

Clay rid himself of his jeans and shoes and then fell back to his knees with her. When they were in the same space once more, their breaths mingling, her breasts brushing against his chest, Clay reached down and grabbed her hand. Her gaze flew to his, her eyes wide because for one crazy moment she thought she'd done something wrong. Clay met her panicked stare evenly, a smug smile tugging at his lips. He brought her hand up and then leaned down, eyes still on Melody as he sucked on the fingers she'd been touching herself with.

Melody took a shuddering breath, her pussy clenching at the implications of that action. She remembered how good it felt to have his tongue on her, licking, sucking, and pushing her to the edge.

"You want it?" Clay asked against the tip of her index finger. He kissed the pad of it, his dark eyes studying her intently. "I'll spread you out on this floor and do it right now."

Melody shook her head. Her pussy was clenching for something more than his tongue. She wanted to connect with him—*she needed it.* There was no way to explain it, but she felt suddenly empty without him. She smiled at him, letting every ounce of longing show on her face as she whispered, "Fuck me instead."

Clay sucked in a sharp breath, his eyes rolling back for one brief moment before he leaned into her. He placed a soft, chaste kiss against her collarbone. "Then stand up. I wanna do you against the glass."

Heat flooded her system. His words set her on fire. She didn't know why, but she wanted this too, something harder, darker, more carnal. Melody craved the forbidden with Clay; she wanted to be dirty with him.

She stood up and turned around, legs spread wide, hands planted over her head against cool glass. She looked out on Las Vegas, the sea of iridescent colors fading out to haloed trails of light without her glasses on. It added to the dreamlike quality of the night, where nothing felt quite real enough or entirely too real to believe.

Still on his knees, Clay pressed a kiss at the base of her spine, his large hands cupping both round globes of her ass. Then he was slowly standing, his lips moving up the line of her back, his hands running over her body, touching her stomach, her hips, squeezing her breasts. By the time he was on his feet, Melody felt surrounded by Clay, hard muscles, strong hands, warm skin. She inhaled the spicy, masculine scent that was uniquely his and closed her eyes against the sea of colors in front of her as she surrendered to the man behind her.

Clay was too tall. This wouldn't have worked if it weren't for the high heels. Even still it took some maneuvering before they found the right position. Clay wrapped one hand around her hip, pulling her back against him, and Melody pressed her cheek against the glass, eyes still closed as she trembled in anticipation.

He guided himself into her, using his hold on her hip to help the thrust. Nothing could ever prepare her for that first push of his cock inside her—it was a dizzying rush every time. Melody took a shuddering breath against the pleasure. He was so big it'd hurt if she wasn't so wet, so incredibly needy. As it was he stretched her, the head of his cock pushing against the spot inside her that Clay had found with his fingers not long ago.

"God," she gasped, trying to breathe past the pleasure. He was moving agonizingly slow, making her feel everything. She curled her fingers against the glass, and her legs shook. She opened her eyes, desperate for a distraction against the ecstasy that was almost too intense. She looked down at the lights once more, forgetting there was ground beneath her. "I think I'm gonna fall."

"I won't let you fall." Clay's voice was tight, making it obvious he was torturing himself with the slow melding of his body into hers. "I promise."

He wrapped one strong arm around her waist, pulling her closer to him just as he thrust hard, forcing Melody to take all of him. The slide of his cock inside of her was harsh, demanding, a stark contrast from the gentle claiming a few seconds ago. She cried out, her body shaking from the current of pleasure. She felt full of him, surrounded by him, and she loved it.

Knowing Clay wouldn't give it to her unless she asked, Melody managed to fight the bliss long enough to choke out one word. "Hard."

Fortunately Clay understood; he pulled out and pushed back in, taking her hard like she'd asked. He groaned in relief, making it obvious this was what he needed too. It felt amazing. The rocket fire of ecstasy gave Melody the thrill of mindlessness she needed. She was desperate to get lost in it, to surrender to every stroke of pleasure.

Still shaking, she fought to find her voice. "Again."

"Fuck," Clay growled, a shudder going over him before he grabbed her hip once more, his grip nearly bruising. His other hand fisted in Melody's hair, tugging her head back as he leaned in and breathed against her ear. "Is this what you want?"

"Yes," Melody choked out, shocking herself as much as him. "I need it. Please."

She never knew she was supposed to be this woman, one comfortable enough with her own body and desires to make herself vulnerable to him like this. She wanted to be claimed, owned, fucked from behind until she came, screaming Clay's name. If she wasn't already in love with Clay, she would have fallen for him just for giving her this freedom. She wasn't nervous and jumpy; instead she was uninhibited and sexual. From the first time she met him, Clay had been slowly freeing her from her past and the stereotypes everyone, even Melody had believed. She could be wild and sexy; she'd just been waiting for Clay to come along and help her blossom into the woman she was always meant to be.

Clay gave her exactly what she needed. He fucked her hard from behind—the position forcing his thick cock to brush against that sensitive place inside her over and over again. Small sobs of pleasure burst out of Melody, and her body shook as the precipice rose.

She would have worried about falling when she was this out of her mind. She surrendered completely to the rise of pleasure, but Clay promised he wouldn't let her fall and she believed him. It gave her free rein to just enjoy the strokes and savor the way Clay sounded as he fucked her. Low grunts of pleasure burst out of him, the tug on her hair and the grip on her waist growing tighter the closer they got to oblivion.

She felt suspended in that place between heaven and hell. The pleasure was all consuming, the attraction between them powerful and irresistible, but the release was beyond her reach. Already completely uninhibited, Melody had no problem reaching between her legs.

"Oh shit," Clay gasped, his hips pushing against hers with another stimulating stroke. He released his tight hold on her hair, his hand slamming against the glass next to her head. "Fuck, you turn me on. Touch yourself. I like that."

Melody rubbed two fingers against her clit. Her head fell back against Clay's shoulder, and she moaned from the dual stimulation. She was going to come. She could feel the climax building to the point that resisting it was almost impossible. She was too turned on, too incredibly grateful to be liberated from past demons, too wanton and free. She fell over the edge, giving in to the flash of pleasure with Clay's name on her lips.

The pulse of her orgasm was consuming. Everything faded to a white haze of bliss. The thrill was electrified when Clay reacted to her coming and pushed her against the glass. He fucked her harder, faster, drawing out Melody's pleasure with every push of his cock into her pussy, which was clenching from the force of her release. Then he tensed behind her, crying out her name with the same feral passion, and shuddered with his own climax. They were lost together, flying over a sea of lights, trapped in the space between, and Melody wanted it to last forever.

But nothing lasted forever.

Melody got a bizarre mental whiplash when the pleasure faded to a hazy hum, jarring her back to reality. She found herself breathless, sagging against the window and blinking at blurred city lights. Clay's arm wrapped around her waist was the only thing keeping her on her feet because her legs had stopped supporting her weight somewhere along the way. Her ankles hurt. Sexy or not, those high heels had to go.

Clay groaned behind her, making it obvious she wasn't the only one feeling the crash from euphoria to reality. "I'm sorry."

"What're you sorry for?" Melody asked, still dazed.

"I was too rough." He pressed a kiss to the top of her head and used his hold on her waist to pull her tighter against him. "I think I'm an asshole."

"Nah," she said, unable to resist grinning. "I liked it. With you, rough works."

"Does it?" he asked, his voice gruff with sex but still hesitant.

"Sure does." Melody's smile grew broader at the realization. "Everything works with you. It's like magic. You make me feel normal, and I love you for it."

Clay was quiet for a long moment before he whispered, "Ditto. Love you too, Mel."

Melody let herself soak it all in, wanting every aspect of this moment committed to memory, even the sticky aftereffects of sex and the dull sting between her legs. She let herself feel the ache in her feet and the knot in her back that came from having a six-five, two-

hundred-and-sixty-pound   heavyweight   champion
draped over her.

The good and bad, she wanted it all, because this
was the moment Melody realized the slots had stopped
spinning. The rush of not knowing was over, but it
wasn't necessarily a bad thing when she considered the
outcome of the gamble.

She'd won.

Chapter Twelve

"Why are they calling it a knockout if he wasn't knocked out?"

Clay looked up from his breakfast, giving her a smile. "It was a technical knockout."

Melody frowned. "What's the difference?"

"The ref calls a technical knockout," Wyatt explained, pointing at her with a sausage at the end of his fork, "'cause, see, Wellings was to the point that he couldn't tap and he was getting clobbered."

"Seems unfair," Melody said, stabbing at her breakfast. They were eating at one of the big buffets that seemed to be everywhere in Las Vegas. Though their hotel was fancier than most, the buffet was casual, which had become a requirement. "What if he could've bounced back?"

"He wasn't bouncing back."

"Ain't no way," Wyatt agreed. "That fight was over five hits before the ref ended it."

"He could've done something. You never know," Melody argued and then took a bite of her eggs, which weren't half bad. She chewed her food, giving Clay a look. "I think it's unfair."

"Well, I can't help you with that." Clay laughed. "I don't make the rules."

"I feel bad for him." Melody sighed, her mind still on the fight. "'Cause you got a whole collection of those tacky belts and he ain't got one."

"That is true." Clay surprised her by agreeing. "If the fates were kind, they'd have probably let Wellings win."

"Are you shitting me?" Wyatt snapped. "That slick bastard's 'bout as cocky as they come."

"And you ain't?" Melody couldn't resist asking.

Clay choked on his food, his face turning red as he coughed and wheezed. Finally a barking laugh burst out of him. He turned to Melody, his eyes watering. "I knew there was a reason I loved you."

"Oh God, I'm gonna puke." Wyatt growled, rolling his eyes at the two of them. "First everyone's fucking jolly for Christmas; now I gotta deal with this. If there's a hell, I'm pretty sure it's got tinsel and a lovesick Clay Powers in it."

"How come you don't like Christmas?" Melody asked curiously.

"'Cause he's hungover," Clay said, still laughing. "Just ignore him."

"He ain't the only one. I should've stayed in bed like Tony and Jasper. I'm 'bout as green as grass in June." Jules sat on Melody's other side, putting her plate in front of her. She leaned in, her arms resting on the table as her voice dropped to a conspiratorial whisper. "Did y'all see Wellings behind you?"

"What?" Wyatt turned around to look at the table behind them. He stiffened, his light eyes narrowing in defensiveness. "Having fun eavesdropping on our conversation?"

"Hard not to. Half the restaurant can hear that big mouth of yours, Conner."

Melody turned around to see Romeo Wellings glaring at them from his seat behind them. Surprisingly he ate alone. Melody wasn't expecting that after glimpsing the big crew of people he'd had with him yesterday at the promotional event he attended with Clay and Wyatt. She hadn't gotten a close look at him the day before, but today she could see the evidence of the fight with Clay, and she winced over it. Between the two of them, Romeo was certainly the worse for the wear.

"Hey, buddy, sorry to bother you." Clay reached out in a rare show of goodwill and hit the back of Romeo's chair. "We'll keep it down."

"Sure." Romeo nodded. His eyes, a light shade of green that was vibrant against his tanned skin, darted to Clay, then to Melody sitting next to him. The tension seemed to slip out of his broad shoulders, and a smile quirked the corner of his mouth. "Keep that one, Powers. She calls it like she sees it; I like that."

Clay grinned back at him. "Yeah, I like that too."

Melody smiled, feeling pleased. They all turned back around, an uncomfortable silence filling the air because they knew Romeo could still hear them. It seemed silly to pretend he wasn't there. So when Melody got up to refill her plate, she leaned down to Romeo.

"I'm happy you're okay," she said with a smile. "I was worried 'bout you."

"Oh yeah, I'm good," he said, giving her an embarrassed laugh. "I got a hard head. I'm a New Yorker; we're all hardheaded and thick-skinned."

"Good to know." She laughed before she turned to go back and get more food.

Even with Melody's attempt at goodwill and Clay being generally ambivalent toward his rival sitting behind them, breakfast wrapped up quicker than it would if it weren't for Romeo listening to everything they were talking about. They didn't have any obligations for the rest of the day, and it was strange for all of them. They walked across the hotel, passing the casino on their way back to the elevator. Aside from sitting in their rooms doing nothing, no one could come up with a good plan of action. Though Clay seemed on board with camping out in the suite, Melody felt like they needed to get out and see something on their last day in Las Vegas.

"We could go Christmas shopping," Melody suggested, feeling excited at the prospect. She had a small stash of money that she'd brought with her. She had been going to use it to set herself up in a new town, but now that she'd decided to stay, Christmas shopping sounded like a much better idea. "Could be fun."

"Who the heck are we gonna shop for?" Wyatt snorted, pulling a face of bemusement at Melody.

Melody stopped, considering that. "Your deputies?"

"I gave 'em gift cards already." Wyatt shrugged. "They count on 'em to do their own Christmas shopping."

"Your employees at the Cellar."

Clay winced, draping his arm over Melody's shoulder. "We give 'em cash."

"Oh." Melody glanced up at Clay and then turned to Jules and Wyatt. They appeared genuinely lost at the idea of Christmas shopping. "Don't y'all buy things for each other at least?"

Jules gave her a look. "Why would we?"

"'Cause it's Christmas." Melody laughed, having never encountered three bigger Scrooges in her entire life. "And ya love each other."

"That's exactly why we ain't gotta buy each other anything," Jules said dismissively. "We could go to a show."

"Pass," Clay said quickly.

"Yeah, I think I'd rather go Christmas shopping for friends and family I ain't got," Wyatt agreed. "Shopping's better than those flashy shows."

"I like 'em," Jules said indignantly. "Maybe Melody'd like one too."

Wyatt huffed and started walking again. "Then you two go."

"If Melody want's to go, then I guess I could go," Clay offered, giving Melody a smile. "I'm spending today with her."

"Then what the heck am I supposed to do while y'all are gone?" Wyatt complained. "Sit in my room jerking off for five hours?"

Jules reached up, smacking the back of Wyatt's head. "Can you pretend you're not a pig?"

"No, I can't," Wyatt said blandly. "I got a headache. I feel like hell."

"I told ya Conners shouldn't drink." Clay grinned, pulling Melody closer and squeezing her arm. "Why don't we try Christmas shopping? It can't be too bad. Maybe I'll buy you two something."

"Maybe," Jules said, casting a sideways glance at her brother. "Maybe I'll buy y'all something too."

"I ain't buying neither of you shit," Wyatt announced, though a smile quirked his lips. "You'll get nothing and like it."

"Well, fuck you, then." Clay laughed.

Wyatt started laughing too. "Fuck you too, you cheesy bastard. I liked ya better ornery."

"Yeah, this is my life," Jules said sadly before a laugh burst out of her. "I've been dealing with this on a daily basis since I was in middle school. Take pity on me."

"I do." Melody laughed with them. "I'm definitely buying you something."

"I'm buying you something just for taking one of 'em off my hands." Jules grinned. "I just gotta change, and we'll take off."

"That works," Clay agreed and then kicked at Wyatt's shin, getting him to make a sound that seemed like a reluctant agreement.

Melody couldn't remember the last time she'd felt this lighthearted. She looked down at herself to study another new dress, this one black with vibrantly colored paisleys running up the side of it. It was lower cut than she usually wore, but she was feeling a bit wild today and decided it was more than acceptable, especially with—

"Oh!" Melody turned, looking back to the direction of the restaurant. "I left my shawl at the table."

"I'll go back and get it," Clay offered.

"No, I'm already dressed," Melody said, slipping out from under Clay's arm. "Y'all go up and get changed, and I'll meet you at the room."

"We could go with—"

"Don't be silly." Melody turned to leave before Clay insisted on following her and slowing their progress. "I'll run."

Melody dashed back toward the restaurant, hoping no one took her shawl. She'd be really disappointed to lose it when it was one of the few nice things she currently owned. Fortunately she wore flats today. If she rushed, she might meet them back at the elevators, because this hotel was truly huge. Walking from end to the other took forever.

"Hey, lady, forget something?"

Melody turned around, looking to her purse on her arm, wondering if something fell out. "I don't think—" She glanced up, staring at the man who'd followed her around the corner from the casino, and gasped. "Justin!"

Icy-cold fear sank into her veins as she stood there staring at her ex-husband for one stunned second. He looked terrible, nothing like the handsome man she'd married. His blond hair was long and stringy, his light eyes wide and crazed. He was thinner and unshaved. He seemed to radiate a dark cruelty. His insides had finally caught up with his outsides, and it didn't paint a pretty picture. He didn't just appear malicious; he seemed unstable in a way he hadn't before, as if he'd lost all hope.

She forced her lungs to suck in air and her brain to start working. She looked wildly behind her, knowing Clay was just around the corner. She gasped when Justin reached out and grabbed her arm.

"I asked if you forgot something?" Justin growled at her, his eyes narrowed menacingly. "'Cause it looks like you're slumming around this hotel like a bitch in heat with that big, dumb hick when you're supposed to be home taking care of me. You're *my wife*. You swore you'd love, honor, and obey me. I'm here to make sure you keep that promise."

"We're divorced." Melody straightened her back and glared at her ex-husband, wondering how she'd put up with this sad, pathetic man for five years. "You'll never get me outta this hotel. I will scream my head off. Just leave before you end up spending Christmas in jail."

"No, I don't think I will." Justin lifted up his shirt, forcing Melody to look down against her will. Her stomach lurched when she saw the glint of metal and the grim smile of promise on his face. "Remember saying 'till death do us part'? One way or the other, you're keeping those vows, Melody, and it doesn't make a difference to me which one. I have no problem blowing your brains out and leaving you for the big bastard to find. So go ahead and scream; maybe you two can die together."

Melody looked around the casino, feeling trapped in one of those horrible news stories. She could already see the headlines: three days before Christmas, a madman shoots up a casino in a jealous rage over his ex-wife. Didn't those things happen all the time? Wasn't this the very reason Melody avoided watching the news like the plague? She was tomorrow's news, and there wasn't a damn thing she could do about it.

She had all these thoughts as Justin pulled her away. Her feet dragged. She couldn't willingly walk to her demise, but she didn't fight. She couldn't help staring at every person she passed, thinking of stray bullets and brutal headlines. She thought of Clay and what he'd do if he walked up on them. She looked wildly for a security guard or some sort of police figure who could possibly help.

"Imagine my surprise when Charlie called me up saying he saw you draped all over one of those big wrestlers on pay-per-view." Justin growled, sounding disgusted. "I always knew you were a whore."

"He's not a wrestler," Melody corrected him, her feet still dragging. She knew she looked like a very unwilling companion, and she hoped that helped. Maybe someone would call the police. "He's a Mixed Martial Arts fighter."

"Same difference. It's all fake."

Feet still dragging, Melody looked behind her, hoping to the catch the eye of someone who could call for help. To distract him more than anything, she argued. "I-it's not fake."

Her teeth were chattering in fear, but she wasn't going to let him get her into a car and somewhere private, because she had no doubt she'd end up dead if she did. The second she could run without risking others getting shot, she was going to chance it, bullet or not.

"Hey, don't I know you?"

Melody turned from her frantic search for help and found her face literally planted in a chest easily as big as Clay's. She tilted her head back and gawked when she realized she was staring at Romeo Wellings.

"Fuck off!" Justin growled.

Head tilted way back, Justin stared up at the man who'd stopped his escape. Then he threw his chest out in a false sense of bravado as his eyes narrowed at Romeo, who was truly intimidating up close and personal. He reminded Melody of one of the guys from those bloody mafia movies—only bigger.

Obviously unnerved by Romeo being completely in their faces, Justin jerked Melody's arm so hard she stumbled. Romeo grabbed her before she could fall. His large hand wrapped around her other arm. His grip was viselike, making it obvious he didn't plan to let go. She shook her head silently at him, thinking of the gun and how truly unstable Justin had become, but Romeo ignored her.

"No, man, no," Romeo said, his New York accent extra thick as he shook Melody's arm, pulling her closer to him. "I know this chick. I seen her somewheres before. Where do I know you?"

Melody gaped at him, wondering if he was being serious. Her eyes were wide in silent warning. She was starting to believe Wyatt's claims that Romeo wasn't just cocky but a little bit crazy as well. He was standing so close, as if he had no respect for personal space, and she could tell it was making Justin twitchy.

"Look at her; this girl's beautiful." Romeo gestured to Melody, pulling her farther from Justin until she was practically tucked under his muscular arm. "How'd a bum like you get a girl like this? And look at that: she's got a hickey. No way you gave that to her, man. I don't fucking believe it."

Justin looked to Melody's neck, his light eyes narrowed in raw rage for one heartbeat. Then Melody felt the brush of air and caught a flash of color. It wasn't until she heard the crunch of bone against fist that Melody realized Romeo had punched him with a speed and velocity that seemed almost inhuman. The blood was shocking because there was so much of it as Justin stumbled, his hands flying to his nose.

"He's got a gun!" Melody screamed.

She was terrified Romeo was going to end up shot, but she hadn't gotten the words out before she was falling, her knees giving way when Romeo took off running in the opposite direction, dragging Melody with him. She realized he wasn't going to stop. He was taking her with him whether she was willing or not. She scrambled to find her feet. Her shoulder burned from the force Romeo used to pull her away before she'd known they were making a run for it.

Melody was dimly aware of the casino breaking out in chaos. Her and Romeo's dash cleared an open path in front of them. People seemed to scatter and fall away like dominoes. The noise was a dull rush behind the fear. She didn't hear anything until one heart-stopping yell, terrifying in its intensity, reached over the chaos and resonated with her.

"MEL!"

Melody looked wildly to the side, seeing Clay coming up on them. She didn't have time to wonder if he'd decided to follow her to the restaurant or if the pandemonium had sent him after her. His eyes were wild as he reached Melody and Romeo, stopping their flight because he was the only one crazy enough to run to them instead of away.

Romeo shouted when they were pulled up short, "Run, Powers!"

"What the hell—"

"It's Justin!"

Melody finally broke Romeo's hold to turn around and look behind her. She managed to catch a glimpse of Justin behind them. He'd been chasing them, which explained the wide berth and the insanity. Out of the corner of her eye, Melody thought she saw men in uniform, but her eyes narrowed in on Justin, who swung the gun wildly in their direction.

"You're gonna fucking die, cunt!"

A loud *pop*.

Glass exploded everywhere.

Clay shoved Melody hard enough that her legs gave out. Her knees hit the floor, the stun of pain making her eyes open wide. Her hands flattened against broken glass to keep herself from landing face-first on the tile. Her scream of fear and pain was trapped in her chest when she suddenly found herself crushed under a solid wall of muscle.

"Clay, no!"

Another *pop* reverberated over the clang of slot machines.

Melody opened her eyes, feeling like she was caught in a nightmare when she blinked to see Clay charge Justin, who still held out the gun. Strangely fearless, Clay dived at him with raw rage that was terrifying. The sound their bodies made as they hit was ghastly, especially when Melody saw the crack of Justin's head hitting the tile. Then Clay's fist was driving into his face, and it was a horrible, bloody sight Melody wanted to look away from and couldn't.

There was no referee to save Justin, and Clay's punches were fast and vicious. Melody realized she was watching him beat Justin to death. She was just going to close her eyes against it when Wyatt skidded on his knees next to the fight and grabbed Clay's fist midair.

"You got him!" Wyatt screamed, struggling to get Clay off Justin. "He's out! STOP!"

Wyatt threw his shoulder into Clay, physically throwing him off Justin. The two huge men landed hard on the tile next to Justin's prone body. Wyatt wrestled with Clay, forcing him onto his back and shouting in that booming sheriff's voice of his, "It's over! Damn it, Clay! It's fucking over!"

Melody wanted to believe it, and Wyatt's speech had a grim certainty that was easy to believe when he used his lawman voice. She stopped watching the wrestling match between the two friends to look for the gun. She found it lying a few feet from Justin's open, unmoving hand.

"That's the difference between a technical knockout and a real one." Romeo panted over her. "I think that fucker's dead."

She might have said something if she could breathe. As it was she grunted and pushed her elbow back against his chest. In the craziness, Romeo hadn't exactly been gentle in his tackle, and she was feeling the full force of having a heavyweight crushing her to tile covered in broken glass. Romeo climbed off her, and Melody sucked in a sharp breath. Her heart was beating the hell out of her ribs. White spots were actually dancing in her vision from the adrenaline pumping through her bloodstream.

Melody was dizzy. She was likely bleeding because her knees and hands stung like they'd been ripped open. All she could think about was Clay. In that moment, her mind wasted very little time on Justin's prone form. If he was dead, so be it.

She scrambled to her feet, her shoe catching on a wet spot and slipping. She *was* bleeding, but she didn't have time to worry about it. The chaos seemed to suck back in on them. Before everyone ran away; now there were people everywhere. Men dressed in uniforms tried to grab her, but she pushed away from their help.

She ran to where Wyatt sat straddled over Clay. They were both breathing hard. Clay's eyes were closed, his jaw clenched, but that wasn't what she really saw. Instead she saw his torso, bared from Wyatt shoving his T-shirt way up. The broad expanse of his chest, his stomach, his shoulders were all coated in blood, and more seemed to be flowing out. Red stickiness gushed from beneath Wyatt's big hands that were pressing hard, as if he could will the bleeding to stop with nothing more than strength and prayer.

"We need an ambulance." Wyatt was panting, only now Melody saw it was sheer panic stealing his voice as he turned and looked wildly to the police officers crowding around them. His face was pale, his eyes wide and terrified. "He's shot."

"No!" Melody felt a cry come somewhere deep in her chest when Wyatt's words hit home. She fell down on her knees next to Clay and stared at his face, which looked pallid and strained. "Clay, no! This isn't fair!"

"Hey." Clay's eyes snapped open, and he reached out, grabbing Melody's thigh through her dress. "I'm okay."

Melody shook her head, feeling light-headed from the fear. Tears stung her eyes, and she was forced to squint. She'd lost her glasses somewhere along the way. The tears just made it harder to see him, and she fought against them. "I don't think you're okay."

"We need an ambulance!" Wyatt screamed again, his big hands still pressing hard against the space between Clay's shoulder and his chest. "Where the hell's the ambulance?"

"I'm fine. It's over now, and we're *both* gonna be fine." Clay squeezed her leg once more. His touch anchored her against the noise and buzz of fear. People crowded around them, looking past the group of police and security with morbid curiosity. Melody made herself blind to everything but Clay's dark eyes holding hers. She heard only his smooth, even voice as he said, "I promise."

Melody reached out and grabbed his hand, still warm and strong. She squeezed it and whispered, "I believe you."

Epilogue

"On a scale of one to ten—one being a normal human reaction and ten being the stupidest fucking thing you could possibly do—jumping at a guy who's got a gun and a vendetta against you for doing his ex-wife has gotta be a twenty-nine."

"Shut up, Wyatt. I'm sick of hearing ya bitch at me 'bout Vegas." Clay stabbed at the ham on his plate, cursing the clumsiness of trying to eat with his left hand. "I'm done with this stupid sling. I don't even need it."

"But the doctors—"

"I don't give a shit what the doctors said!"

Clay struggled with the sling. He pulled it over his head and knocked his cap off in the process. He tossed both to the bench next to him and then picked up his fork with his right hand. His shoulder ached with the movement, but after three days of eating with his left hand, he didn't give a fuck.

"Melody's gonna have your ass."

"Probably," Clay agreed, looking past the booth to see Melody at the counter, waiting for her order to come up. "I guess that'll make us even. I'm not real thrilled she's working just 'cause she promised Mary she'd cover her Christmas Eve shift. Her hands are still full of stitches."

Wyatt winced. "How's her shoulder?"

"Eh, it's all right, not great." Clay shrugged and took another bite of his dinner. "You know Romeo 'bout jerked her arm outta the socket. Doctor said she tore some muscles. It'll probably ache for ages."

"Did you really offer to be his training partner?" Wyatt asked with a dark scowl.

"Yes, I really offered to be his training partner." Clay gave Wyatt a look, not understanding why it was such a shock. "I'm retiring. He needs to work on skill sets I'm strong in. There ain't no reason why he can't use the Cellar for his training camp."

"He's got a criminal record."

"I don't give a shit," Clay said with a laugh of disbelief. "We can't all be Conner perfect."

"I think his family's mafia."

"Why, 'cause he's from New York? You gotta stop watching those movies."

"I been checking round. I got sources. This ain't me being paranoid. I have legitimate facts, Clay," Wyatt told him, his eyes narrowed with lawman intensity. "That boy's got a rap sheet and a questionable family. I think you're bringing organized crime right into the heart of Garnet by inviting him here."

"Well, that ain't my problem," Clay said dismissively. "All I know is Romeo saved Mel's life and if he needs a training partner, I'm more than happy to help him out. It's the least I can do. Besides I don't think Romeo or organized crime gives a rat's ass 'bout Garnet even *if* there's something fishy going on with him."

"There is something fishy. I'm right 'bout this. Y'all are gonna be apologizing to me."

"I'm 'bout over this conversation. Ain't there laws being broken somewhere?"

"Probably." Wyatt sighed, taking a sip of his coffee. "Criminals don't stop for Christmas."

Clay snorted. "Yeah, 'cause we're so overrun with criminals round here."

"It's 'cause I do my job that we ain't," Wyatt snapped at him. "And it'd be nice if ya appreciated it."

"Hey," Melody said, glaring at their booth as she walked past with plates in both hands. "Where's your sling?"

"Where's yours?" Clay countered.

Melody huffed, rolling her eyes as she delivered dinner to the booth behind them. Clay wasn't pleased she was working, but it was slow. Not many people were eating at Hal's Diner on Christmas Eve. It actually reminded Clay of Thanksgiving, and he found himself feeling nostalgic as Melody stopped at their booth.

"You gonna buy me a piece of pie?" he asked her, giving her a grin he hoped distracted from the sling argument.

"I might." Melody gave him a reluctant smile as she sat next to him in the booth. "How's your dinner?"

"It's good." Clay held out his fork. "You want some?"

"I've been snacking in the back." Melody accepted the fork and took a quick bite. She chewed her food, her eyebrows going up in surprise. "I'm not usually fond of yams, but these ain't half bad."

"Ain't half bad at all," Clay agreed. "I don't know why more folks don't just eat here on holidays. Better than dried up ol' turkey and boxed stuffing."

"Probably 'cause they got families." Melody laughed, taking another bite of his food. Then she glanced up at Wyatt, who was staring at the two of them with a look of revulsion on his face. "What's got you looking miserable?"

"This really happened, didn't it?" Wyatt asked, shaking his head as he watched Melody eat off Clay's plate. "You two are gonna end up getting married and having a buncha babies and living happily ever after. I could puke."

Melody choked. A hand flew to her chest as she looked to Clay with wide eyes.

"Don't panic. He's just being dramatic," Clay said by way of explanation as he reached across the table and picked up Wyatt's unused roll of silverware. "He does that sometimes. He thinks Romeo's part of an organized crime family too."

Melody laughed. "He does talk like one of those guys in the movies, but he's sweet. I like Romeo."

"Well, I guess." Clay stabbed at another piece of ham with his new fork since Melody seemed intent on finishing off his yams. "He did save your life."

"He did," Melody agreed. "I got the sore shoulder to prove it."

"Is it really bothering you?"

"It's all right. I took an aspirin."

"What about your hands?" Clay reached for her hand, still holding a fork, and studied it. She wore thin, black gloves to protect the still-healing stitches. "Why dontcha take these off. Lemme look at 'em."

"They're fine." Melody turned to him, her eyes narrowed. "Why aren't you wearing that sling? I got a few cuts and a pulled muscle; you got a *bullet hole* in you."

"It didn't hit anything," Clay said dismissively. "They dug it out, and I was fine."

"It coulda hit something," Wyatt reminded him. "It was a fucking miracle it didn't. You wouldn't be so bright-eyed and bushy tailed with a bullet in your heart."

Clay felt Melody stiffen next to him, and he was tempted to reach across the booth and dent Wyatt a little—or a lot.

Instead he rubbed Melody's leg through her uniform, squeezing her thigh to reassure her. "I'm okay, Mel. I'm healthy."

She nodded, her eyes still wide beneath her glasses as she took a shuddering breath. "I know."

"Soon as he gets outta the hospital, Justin's going to jail for a long time. He's not coming back. It's over."

"What if you'd died?" Melody whispered, eyes still wide and horrified as she stared at the table unseeing.

"I didn't."

"What if he'd shot someone else trying to get at me?"

"He didn't."

"What if they let him off?" Melody lifted her eyes to him in concern. "What if he tries to hurt you again?"

"He shot up a casino full of witnesses and hidden cameras. Half this country's seen video of him putting a bullet in me," Clay said with a bark of laughter. "There ain't no way they're letting him off."

"True." Melody took another deep breath. "I'm so tired of the news. I can't wait for this to blow over."

"The one nice thing 'bout Christmas," Wyatt started thoughtfully, taking a sip of his coffee. "It finally sent all those leeches home for a few days. I'm sick of those reporters and cameramen camping out in Garnet. Ain't there more interesting news in the world?"

"Than two UFC fighters stopping a crazed gunman?" Melody laughed. "Probably not. Clay and Romeo are heroes. People like heroes."

Wyatt rolled his eyes. "You two put a good name on the sport. I'll give ya that. The promoters couldn't pay for publicity like that."

"They want us to go on a tour together." Clay laughed. "Can you imagine? They've been hounding me since I got outta the hospital."

"That's a nightmare." Wyatt laughed with him. "I thought they learned keeping you as far away from the public as possible was the best course of action?"

Clay shrugged. "Guess not. They want me to bring Melody. They think she'll keep me cordial."

Wyatt gave him a look. "And?"

"Hell no," Clay said. "I'm retiring so I don't have to deal with that publicity shit anymore. I love the sport, but I hate the circus. Now I can camp out in the Cellar, teach classes, and die happy. There ain't any amount of money that's gonna change my mind 'bout it."

"How much money did they offer you?" Melody asked curiously.

Clay winced, knowing he'd sound insane if he gave an actual number. "A lot."

"How long's the tour?"

"A couple of weeks, maybe a month."

"Well," Melody started, giving him a look. "A few weeks of your life ain't nothing."

"No," Clay said firmly. "I can't go and smile and pretend I know how to talk to people. I hate that shit."

"But Romeo'd be with you," Melody said thoughtfully. "And he talks 'bout as much as Wyatt. You wouldn't have to say much."

Clay grunted. "No."

"You could do something good with your share of the money," Melody said softly. "Like...open up a women's shelter or something. It could be for charity."

Clay considered that silently, hearing the hope in Melody's voice. He turned to look at her hesitantly. "I dunno, maybe for charity. If you came with me, I *might* do it."

"Really?" Melody beamed, excitement radiating off her out of the blue. "You'll talk to them about it?" she asked hopefully. "I'd go with you. Hal'll give me time off; I'm sure of it."

Clay sighed, knowing he was already defeated. It'd been a trying four days. It was nice to see Melody excited about something. Justin was still in the hospital. The outlook was hopeful now, but for a few days they'd thought he might not make it. Clay suffered through the very real fear that Melody may have watched him beat her ex-husband to death, which was good in theory but horrifying to face in reality.

Even when Justin did finally get out of the hospital, they had a trial to deal with, and Clay wasn't real pleased with the notion of Melody facing Justin in court. They still had obstacles to face. If going on this tour and starting a women's charity kept her mind off it, Clay could pretend he knew how to be polite for a few weeks.

"I'll talk to 'em." Clay gave her a smile. "We'll use the money to set up some sorta charity. It's a lotta money, Mel. You could open more than one women's shelter with it. Jules could start it up fast for us, and maybe they'd promote the tour for your new charity. Makes 'em look good, and that's what they care 'bout."

Melody's eyes grew watery, glittering like emeralds beneath her glasses. "This is my dream, Clay. This is what I wanted to do ever since I first got away from Justin. Are we really gonna do it? Is it really that easy?"

"Absolutely." His smile grew broader. Her excitement was contagious, and he reached out, cupping Melody's face in both his hands. He leaned in and kissed her, speaking against her lips. "We're doing this. I promise."

She hugged him and pressed her lips to his once more, but her smile made it hard to kiss effectively. Clay ran one hand to the back of her neck and pulled her closer. He nipped her bottom lip, hoping she'd part to him and let him kiss her for real.

"Oh hell no," Wyatt snapped. "If you think I'm gonna sit here while you two start making out in lovey-dovey bliss, y'all got another think coming."

"Fine." Melody laughed and pulled away from Clay. "I gotta go back to work anyway."

"Go," Clay said, giving her a playful shove. "Get these folks outta here so we can get home."

"Sounds like a plan." Melody scooted out of the booth. Her smile was still broad and pleased, showing off deep dimples in both cheeks. She smoothed her uniform and then reached out, smacking Wyatt's arm lightly. "Stop sitting there and scowling. Life ain't that bad."

"It's Christmas." Clay laughed at Wyatt's scowl. "Where's that easy charm you've always got?"

Wyatt shrugged as Melody ran back behind the counter. He looked at his coffee. "It's weird at home now that you've moved in with Melody."

Clay smirked. "I didn't know you cared."

"It ain't that." Wyatt sighed. "Just makes me realize I'm thirty-three years old, with no damn prospects, and no hope for anything more than living out my days arguing with Jules."

"Half the women you meet are in love with you," Clay reminded him. "You got more prospects than any guy in Garnet."

Wyatt looked up from his coffee. The charismatic facade falling away left him exposed and vulnerable in a way Clay hadn't seen in years. His eyes were stark with pain as he whispered, "They ain't Tabitha."

"Nope," Clay agreed sadly, feeling his heart hurt for his friend. "They ain't Tabitha, and they'll likely never be. She's gone, Wyatt. She's been gone a long time now. She left, and I can't really blame her for never coming back 'cause this town wasn't ever any good to her. It's probably 'bout time you got over her."

"You stuck around," Wyatt said sullenly, the comparison obvious. Before life left him jaded, Wyatt had a real talent for attracting friends from the wrong side of the tracks. He studied Clay silently, drinking his coffee before he whispered against the rim of his cup, "It turned out all right for you."

"Yeah, but I don't really give a shit what people think of me. They thought I was trash and I never cared," Clay reminded him. "Tabitha cared."

"For you."

Clay looked up when Melody put a piece of praline pie in front of him. Her hair was in a bun, with wisps of blonde hair framing her face. Her blue and white uniform clung to her lush figure. Her black-framed glasses made her bright green eyes seem just a little bit bigger. With the exception of the gloves protecting her injured hands, she looked almost exactly the same as she had the night he met her. The wistfulness hit him in the center of the chest. He could be sitting here miserable with Wyatt like he had every Christmas before, but he wasn't.

He smiled, feeling happy to be where he was, even with a hole in his shoulder and obstacles left to face. "Thanks, Mel."

"No problem." Melody grinned back at him and leaned over to put a piece of pumpkin pie in front of Wyatt. "For you, Sheriff. On the house. That's lucky pumpkin pie."

"I guess." He looked at the pie as a smile tugged at his lips. "Thank you, Melody."

"Merry Christmas," she said as she moved to check on the booth behind them.

Wyatt took a bite of his pumpkin pie, and Clay watched him eat it for a few moments before he said, "You never know, Wyatt. Things could change for you."

Wyatt gave him a look, making it obvious he thought Clay had lost his mind. "You telling me you think a piece of pie's gonna fix my problems?"

"Why not?" Clay laughed. "Fixed mine."

THE END

Kele Moon

A freckle-faced redhead born and raised in Hawaii, Kele Moon has always been a bit of a sore thumb and has come to enjoy the novelty of it. She thrives on pushing the envelope and finding ways to make the impossible work in her storytelling. With a mad passion for romance, she adores the art of falling in love. The only rule she believes in is that, in love, there are no rules and true love knows no bounds.

So obsessed is she with the beauty of romance and the novelty of creating it, she's lost in her own wonder world most of the time. Thankfully she married her own dark, handsome, brooding hero who has infinite patience for her airy ways, and attempts to keep her grounded. When she leaves her keys in the refrigerator or her cell phone in the oven, he's usually there to save her from herself. The two of them now reside in Florida with their three beautiful children, who make their lives both fun and challenging in equal parts—they wouldn't have it any other way.

Read more about Kele and her books at http://www.kelemoon.com.

Loose Id® Titles by Kele Moon

*Available in digital format at http://www.loose-id.com
or your favorite online retailer*

Packing Heat

* * * *

The **BATTERED HEARTS** Series
Defying the Odds

Battered Hearts *is also available in print from your favorite bookseller*

CPSIA information can be obtained at www.ICGtesting.com
Printed in the USA
BVOW021130280912

301676BV00001B/91/P